Also by

Guarding Temptation

Talia Hibbert

Nixon House

Copyright

Cover Design by Qamber Designs
Edited by Kia Thomas Editing

Published by Nixon House
Print ISBN: 978-1-913651-12-1

www.nixonhouse.co.uk

For the pessimists.

Content Note

Guarding Temptation is a cosy, spicy romance with a dash of angst and a guaranteed happy ending. However, this story includes potentially triggering content, such as:

- Death threats
- Online abuse
- Racism
- Sexism
- Corrupt policing.

Please take care of yourself when reading.

Prologue

"**W**e shouldn't have done it."

Nina wanted to tell herself that she'd misheard. That James Foster, her brother's best friend and her actual dream guy, hadn't just said those words thirty seconds after making her come on his sofa. But he was sitting with his elbows resting on his knees, his massive shoulders slumped and his shaven head bowed—which was universal body language for *"Wow, I have so many regrets right now."*

So, she definitely hadn't misheard. Shit.

Her heart dropped, hit the floor, and cracked right in two. She probably should've stayed silent, should've maintained some sort of dignity. But Nina Chapman had been born mouthy, and her twenty-three years of life had only exacerbated the issue. So she leapt to her feet and demanded, "Are you serious?"

James's head snapped up, surprise written all over his handsome face. "You disagree?"

What the *fuck* was that supposed to mean? Like it should be painfully obvious that she was a bad idea, right after he'd licked her to orgasm? Face burning, Nina snatched her jeans up off the

1

floor—where *he'd* dropped them. "At least let me get my clothes on before you start complaining."

"Nina." Now he had the audacity to look upset, his full mouth pressed into a severe line, deep furrows marking his brow. God, he was irritating. And worse, when he stood, she saw the hard-on tenting his suit trousers.

Only James would be wearing suit trousers and a crisp blue shirt on a Sunday morning. Only James would get rid of a woman—after doing that filthy thing he'd done with his tongue while *wearing* said suit trousers!—and seem surprised when she didn't want to leave. As if he honestly had no idea how attractive he was.

And only James could make her think fond thoughts about him even when she wanted to punch him in the face.

Yes, Nina definitely wanted to punch him in the face. Because not only had he made her come, he'd apparently enjoyed it, at least physically. Yet even his unfulfilled desire wasn't enough for him to actually fuck her.

Honestly, it was becoming painfully clear that nothing would be enough to make him fuck her. She'd gone all out with this silly seduction plan, hoping he'd finally see her as *Nina* instead of the kid she'd been back when they first met. Hoping he'd stop treating her like a little sister or a best friend and start treating her like a grown woman. Well, he'd treated her like a woman alright, and look what it got her: battered pride and pitying looks.

At least she thought that was pity in his eyes. It was something bleak and awful, anyway.

"I'm sorry, Cupcake," he said, and the childhood nickname just made everything worse.

"Don't apologise to the woman you just slept with, James. It's very déclassé."

He winced. "We didn't—"

"I recommend you shut the fuck up before I throw you out the window, okay?" It was an empty threat, of course, and not just because she'd never hurt him. Nina wasn't exactly a light-weight, but he had at least a hundred pounds on her. There was no way on God's green earth she could ever throw James fucking Foster out of a window. He knew that, and yet he nodded solemnly and kept quiet.

If all she wanted was to sleep with James, this rejection wouldn't have bothered her. There were plenty of guys she could sleep with, plenty of guys she *did* sleep with. But none of those men were sweet and serious and generous and open and determined and protective and *James*. None of those men had gone from being her brother's best friend, just part of the furniture, to someone she might actually—nauseatingly—love.

Maybe this whole thing had been doomed from the start anyway. Nina knew very little about love, which was why her reaction to it had been a mortifying attempt at seduction rather than, say, a heart-to-heart.

She'd take this romantic failure as a sign, she decided. Clearly, this wasn't meant to be.

Her expression grim, she shoved on her boots and patted her pockets, making sure her phone and keys were there.

"Don't go," James said. As always, his deep voice held a tone of command. Which, as always, made her determined to ignore him. "I need to talk to you, Nina. We—" He broke off, which was odd enough to make her pause. James usually spoke like a statesman. He did not hesitate and he did not stutter. But he recovered quickly, and she was too pissed to wonder about it. "We need to talk," he finished, kind of redundantly.

"Don't worry," she gritted out. "I won't tell my brother."

He actually flinched at the last word. Then he shut his eyes, ran a hand over his jaw and sighed, "Ah, shit. Markus."

Well, holy fucksticks in a bleeding blue canoe. He hadn't

even *thought* about her brother. He hadn't pulled the brakes because of anything to do with Mark's protective instincts, or some weird bro-code, *don't-sleep-with-my-little-sister thing*, or because years ago, when Mark joined the Royal Air Force, he'd asked James to "look after" her.

James really just straight-up didn't want her. At all.

Great.

She strode out of the room.

"Nina!"

"Nina, sweetheart, you're so fucking wet, let me taste you, I need to taste you ..."

She pushed the painfully fresh memory—the *lie*—away and practically ran through the flat. He followed her, of course. He'd never let her disappear when she was upset. He was way too fucking nice for that.

God, she hated nice.

She wrenched open James's front door, then turned to face him. The sight of him was like a slap. Somehow, despite the fact that his actions had made her all cold and hard inside, he didn't look different at all. He was still gorgeous, with his gentle eyes and strong jaw and full lips—God, those lips—and his soft, bear-like bulk that she wanted to sink into ...

But wouldn't, ever again.

"Nina," he said, "I'm not explaining this very well. I'm sorry."

The apology tore through her flesh like a blade. She blinked, her eyes stinging with something hot and prickly that surely couldn't be tears. *Surely.* God, she couldn't let him see that she was on the edge of crying. The only thing more embarrassing than what had just happened would be James knowing how deeply it hurt.

He could never, ever know how deeply it hurt.

Her words rapid and desperate, her nails carving into the

palms of her hands, she lashed out. "If you really don't want to upset me, James, then don't talk to me. Ever. I don't want to see you. I don't want to hear from you. Unless my brother's home and we have to play nice, stay the fuck away from me. Please."

He stared at her with a sort of devastated horror, his umber skin taking on a greyish tinge. He looked so unhappy, she actually had to fight the instinct to comfort him, which was ridiculous. He was a grown man, for one thing, seven years older than she was. And anyway, what the fuck did he have to be upset about?

Nothing. Absolutely nothing.

Message delivered, she stepped out into the hall and slammed the door shut in his face.

Chapter One

Six Weeks Later

"Heads up." Benny grinned. "Shadow's here."

James tensed, staring blankly at the carburettor in front of him. "*Shadow*" was his technician's nickname for Nina. But she hadn't been James's shadow for a long while now.

Actually, it had been well over a month since he'd ruined everything between them. But somehow, it felt like forever.

He bent deeper under the bonnet of the Morris Minor he was working on and ignored Benny's bullshit. The guy was notorious for his "practical jokes"; no doubt James's employees wanted to see how pathetically eager he'd become if he thought Nina was around. Well, he wouldn't give them the satisfaction. It was obvious to anyone who knew him that he was miserable without her. They didn't need to know any more than that.

"Big man," Benny called. "You hear me?"

Unfortunately, yes. Gritting his teeth, James stayed silent and attacked a rusted-on bolt. The classic car had been ... neglected, and now even penetrating oil didn't seem to be helping. He didn't mind, though. In fact, he'd taken on this job as a favour for his dad's old mate because the force it required was an excellent distraction. He threw himself into the task, letting physical exertion pull him away from his near-constant thoughts of Nina.

Then an achingly familiar voice hit him, harsh and flat and music to his fucking ears. "You busy or what?"

He straightened up so fast, he smacked his head on the Moggie's bonnet. "*Shit.*" Holding a hand to his now-throbbing skull, James emerged from under the hood with a scowl. But the expression melted away when he realised his ears hadn't deceived him—and neither had Benny. Nina was here. Standing just three feet away and glaring at him like he'd eaten her firstborn.

Her hair was shoved on top of her head in a knot, her heavy-lidded eyes were shadowed, and her jaw was tight. Her clothes were oversized, fraying, and entirely black. She looked like heaven. And if things were different—if he weren't such a thick-headed *dick*—he could be throwing an arm over her shoulders and taking her to lunch right about now. James wiped his oily hands on his coveralls and lowered the bonnet. Calm. He would stay calm. He was always calm.

Only she ever threatened his peace. Only she could ever make him wild.

"I'm never too busy for you," he said.

She huffed out something too bitter to be a laugh, turned on her heel, and stomped off in the direction of his office.

Things were rarely easy with Nina. But they were always worth it.

"I'm getting death threats," she said.

James blinked. His mind, usually so smooth and methodical, ground to an abrupt halt. He used the lull in mental activity to stare at her—to devour her, in fact, all the tiny details he'd missed so fucking much. She was bold and beautiful in the grimy little afterthought that was his private office, sitting in her uncomfortable spindly seat as if it were a throne. Around her, everything was exactly as it should be. His old wooden desk had a huge chipped dent in it where he'd once dropped a wrench. The paperwork strewn about was stained with engine oil that he hadn't quite wiped off his palms. The tiny black-and-white CCTV monitor in the corner was playing crackly footage. There was nothing to suggest that he'd recently fallen into another dimension or that he was currently experiencing a mild stroke.

Which meant that he'd heard her correctly.

"Death threats," James repeated, his mind lurching back to life.

"Yes," she said, utterly expressionless. "Death threats. Definition: a typically anonymous threat made by a person or group of people regarding the planned murder of another person or group of people, usually—"

"Nina, stop it." He ran a rough hand over his jaw, barely feeling the rasp of his own stubble. Barely feeling anything. His pulse raced as the implications sank in. Death threats? Nina? *Who the fuck ...?* But losing his temper wouldn't help. She hadn't come to him because she needed a big strong man to punch a hole through the nearest wall; she'd come to him, presumably, for help. So James shoved down the volcanic explosion inside him and tried to stay focused. Detached. Logical. Even though his primary instinct, right now, was to wrap her in his arms and never let go.

That is not an option. Move on.

"Alright," James said briskly, thinking fast. "I'm assuming this has something to do with the site?"

"Yep."

Nina was the anonymous founder and editor of *Reality*

Check UK, an independent political news site dedicated to explaining current events, human rights, and British law in a manner that average citizens could understand. Her work ... upset certain people. To say the least. Nina was, supposedly, a radical. But most of the things she believed seemed like common sense to James.

"My article about Brexit's Leave campaign breaking electoral law went viral," she said. "Millions of hits. *The Sun* called me a Black rights extremist."

He frowned. "What does the Leave campaign have to do with—"

Nina rolled her eyes, waving a hand tipped with chipped black nails. "Don't try to make it make sense. It's *The Sun.*"

Fair point. James's temper rose again at the thought of Nina targeted by that rag. She'd had minor issues before, angry commenters and fascist trolls, but this ... A thought, a glimmer of memory, struck him, cutting through the anger. "Wait. You published that Leave article, what, a month back?"

For the first time all day, her face betrayed a fragment of emotion, barely enough for most people to decode. But he'd met Nina when she was a permanently disgusted teenager heavy into her Goth phase; she couldn't hide from him. He understood the slight flicker of her lashes, the way her direct gaze darted away for a moment. She was shocked. Apparently, she hadn't expected him to keep up with her work while they weren't speaking.

He had no idea why. They'd gone from texting constantly and talking every day to absolute silence. He'd read more of her website in the past six weeks than he had over the last two years, just because he wanted to feel like he was with her. Which was probably pathetic. But not as pathetic as the fact that he'd been driving by her house every night just to check she was okay.

Her brother *had* asked James to keep an eye on her, after all.

Though Mark probably wouldn't approve of just how hard James had been looking recently.

"I published the piece a while ago," Nina hedged, which was a non-answer if he'd ever heard one.

He took a deep breath, because he had a feeling he'd need to concentrate on staying calm during this conversation. "And the death threats started *when?*"

"A few weeks back," she mumbled.

So much for staying calm. James stood up so fast, his chair hit the floor with a harsh *clang.* She jumped slightly, but he couldn't even bring himself to care. He was too busy trying not to breathe fire, the sudden fury in his chest burned so hot and bright. "*Weeks,* Nina? Are you serious?"

She folded her arms, glaring up at him. "Sit down. You look like a bloody brick wall."

He ignored her, planting his hands flat on the desk and leaning forward. "You've been getting death threats for weeks, and I'm hearing about this *now?*"

Her cheeks hollowed, which meant she was biting down on the insides. Hard.

Little hurts. She was always hurting herself. He hated it. But he had hurt her too, hadn't he? He'd made a decision he wasn't ready to deal with, touching her, and when it all got too real and he came to his senses, he'd pushed her away.

Funnily enough, women didn't like to be pushed away during sex. Maybe if he hadn't been dizzy with ill-advised horniness at the time, he would've remembered that and been more tactful.

Or refused to touch her in the first place, genius.

"It's not like I could tell you before," she said, dragging him out of depressingly familiar thoughts.

His blood became ice. "You mean you kept this to yourself just because we aren't talking?"

"I mean why the fuck would I tell you anything when we aren't friends anymore?" she shot back. Every word was like a bullet, slamming into him and tearing him apart. *"We aren't friends anymore."* Is that what she thought? Is that what this was? He'd told himself that if he gave her space, things would all work out in the end. But what if he'd been wrong? He'd also told himself that she'd spoken in anger on that awful day, but Nina was never carried away by emotion like he was.

What if she'd meant every fucking word?

The fire in him burned out, leaving nothing but cold, charred insides behind. James felt suddenly disorientated, as if the world had shifted around him. But he couldn't waste time with self-indulgent worries about his place in Nina's life when that life was apparently in danger.

And you weren't there for her. She's been dealing with this alone for weeks, all because you were weak.

He squashed the guilt. It could haunt him later.

"If you weren't planning on coming to me," he said quietly, "what changed? Did something happen?"

Her silence was even more damning than her suddenly shifty gaze.

"*Nina.* What. Happened?"

She exhaled sharply, slumping down in her seat. One booted foot came up to rest against his desk, and she fiddled with the rip in her jeans. "I thought—I mean, I was wrong, I'm sure I was wrong—but I *thought* I heard somebody trying to get into the house last night."

His lungs seized. "Explain."

"Well, now it's daylight, I think I was just paranoid. But I got a few weird tweets yesterday, cryptic comments about figuring out my identity, you know? Like someone knew who I was. And then, last night, I heard the front door rattling. It was probably the wind, but—"

"What?" he choked out. A cocktail of anger and fear held his muscles in its tight, clawed grip. "Why didn't you call me?"

Her mulish stare was apparently all the answer she was prepared to give.

"Did you at least call *someone*?" he demanded.

"Like who? Flynn? Jasmine? *Hey, babes, come over and make sure I'm not murdered, would you? Bring Jelly Babies. Xoxo, Nina.*"

"Like the *police*," he gritted out.

"Hmm ... home alone with a stalker, or home alone with the police. What an exciting game of chance."

James closed his eyes and took yet another deep breath. He knew Nina distrusted the police more than most, thanks to her past experiences with them. It was interesting, how often peaceful protests ended with her behind bars. And how frequently whatever charge they'd dragged her in on later proved to be absolute bullshit.

"Fine," James conceded, opening his eyes again. "Fine. Okay. But you do realise that we need to report this, right?"

She gave him a dark look.

"Nina."

"Yes," she said flatly. "I realise that."

"Good. Okay. We'll do it together. I'll take you to the station."

"Not right now," she said.

He stared. "I really think we should deal with this as quickly as possible."

Her tongue snaked out to wet her lips. She turned her head to stare at the CCTV screen. He followed her gaze and found nothing unusual. So, she wasn't distracted; she was deflecting. Which, combined with her uncharacteristic meekness, added up to one thing: Nina was nervous.

"Alright," he said. "Not yet. Tomorrow. We'll spend today

focusing on ... other things." Things that would make her feel better, safer, more like herself. "Starting with taking down the website."

She jerked back to face him. "Get fucked."

"I'm serious."

"So am I. They *want* me to shut the site down, James. That's why they're doing this, and it would be an easy out, but I can't. I can't give them that kind of power and I can't forfeit my principles. I won't be silenced."

The speech pissed him off, but at least she was starting to sound like her usual self: loud, uncontainable, generally annoyed at the world. He liked her passion. He *loved* her passion. But he'd wished, more than once, that she'd put herself before the good of "society".

"Nina, I know your work is important—"

"Do you?" she demanded, lifting her chin.

"*Yes*," he insisted. "I do. But it's not more important than your safety. If whoever's threatening you wants you to take the site down—"

"I comply?" she interrupted softly. "You know how I feel about compliance, James."

He did. In fact, he usually agreed with her. He was struggling now, caught between his own beliefs, the promise he'd made to her brother, and the way he felt about her.

On the one hand, he knew that the world would be a shit-storm if people like them sat back and did as they were told. On the other hand, his best friend had asked him to watch over Nina while he was off engineering Her Majesty's sodding death-planes with the RAF. And since she'd been nineteen at the time, James had agreed. But Nina wasn't a kid anymore, and somehow, he'd started to see her differently. Very differently.

Which brought him to the metaphorical third hand: he would rather gnaw off his own arm than ever see Nina hurt, or even unhappy. If he had a choice between saving the planet from alien invasion and saving *her* ... Well, he should choose saving the planet. He knew that. But he also knew that he would definitely, one hundred per cent, without remorse, choose her.

Which probably wasn't healthy, and definitely wasn't an attitude conducive to his *stop-being-in-love-with-Nina* plan.

So he forced himself to say, "Fine. You're right. The site stays. For now."

She arched her brows slightly, a sharp almost-smile curving her lips. It didn't mean she was happy. It meant she was basking in her own dominance, or some such Nina-like bullshit. But the sight of any expression on her face made his heart swell with hope, because blankness was her defence mechanism. If she *wasn't* blank, she was letting him in. Whether she realised it or not.

Fighting a smile of his own, James started to pace. "Next up: living arrangements. You can't go home."

"Believe me," she said dryly, "I have no desire to."

If things were the way they used to be, he'd touch her right now. He'd take her hand for a moment, ease her clenched fist open to reveal her ink-stained palm. He'd trace her life line up to her wrist, then run a finger over her racing pulse until it calmed. Once it did, he'd pull her into a hug, and she'd let herself be afraid. She'd whisper her feelings into his ear like they were dirty secrets, and he'd protect them for her like precious stones.

But things weren't the way they used to be, and he was beginning to think that the line they'd crossed six weeks ago was something they could never undo. Things had changed, and he needed to figure out what that meant. But one thing was for certain. Whether she liked him or not, whether she wanted to hug him or kick him in the nuts, Nina was his to protect. So, despite the confused mess of his thoughts, he spoke without hesitation. "You'll stay with me."

"Like fuck," she snorted.

James sighed. He wasn't in the habit of telling Nina what to do, but he could, and he would. "I know you like to argue—"

"Now you're just *trying* to piss me off."

"—but this really isn't up for debate."

She twirled a stray curl around her finger and batted her eyelashes. "Is this the part where I say 'Yes, Daddy,' and do as I'm told?"

James ignored the many layers of sarcasm in that sentence. He also ignored the entirely disturbing way it made his dick jump. This was his usual tactic when it came to Nina's teasing and Nina's strength and Nina's beautiful fucking face: ignoring it.

Instead of throwing her over his shoulder and dragging her kicking and screaming to the safety of his flat—which was what he *wanted* to do—he took a deep breath, walked around the desk, and leaned against it, facing her. He met her flinty gaze and held it, letting her see his worry, his outright fear.

And then, when the hard set of her jaw softened and her scowl faded slightly, he said, "How would you feel, Nina? If I wasn't safe in my own home?"

She huffed out a sigh and rolled her eyes haughtily, and he knew she was cracking. "Don't ask me emotional questions. We aren't friends."

He didn't flinch, focused on his goal. "Who's going to keep you safer than me?"

She tutted. "Because you're a tank who spent years learning to beat the shit out of people, you mean?"

Despite everything, James managed to laugh at her phrasing. "I assume you're talking about my kickboxing days." Not that he'd exactly given up his sport; he'd just stopped bothering to compete. Didn't matter. His father had made him start lessons years ago because *"A boy needs something to do, and men our size need to understand and respect our own strength."*

And now James was going to understand and respect his own strength into someone's skull if they fucked with Nina and made it necessary. Simple.

"Whatever," she sighed. "It's not your job to keep me safe."

"But I'm going to do it anyway. No need to thank me." Trying not to smile at her outraged expression, James stood and strode toward the door. "We'll get your stuff after I close up."

"What are you going to do?" she growled. "Kidnap me?"

"If necessary, Cupcake."

"You wouldn't dare."

She wasn't seriously arguing anymore, he could tell. She knew he was right, and she'd already given in. Still, he responded honestly. "For you, I'd dare a lot."

Chapter Two

The fact that Nina had given in to James didn't make her fickle, or pathetic, or childish—at least that's what she assured herself as she flopped back against his bed and stared at the ceiling. She was afraid, she was at risk, and she had limited options so far as the whole "feeling safe" thing went. That was all.

This didn't mean she'd forgiven him for ... well, for the disgraceful crime of not being in love with her, which wasn't technically a crime, but whatever. Nor did it mean she'd given up on her personal resolution to stop being in love with *him*. Three years of unrequited adoration was more than enough. She was a dignified sort of woman, after all.

But burying herself in James's sheets was making it hard to remember all that, and even harder to focus on disliking him. The scent of clean skin and star anise, along with the hint of engine-oil-edged musk that was pure James, flooded her lungs and confused her heart. How the fuck was she supposed to sleep in here, like he'd insisted?

About as easily as he'd manage to sleep on the sofa, probably. The thought of him squashing his broad frame onto living room furniture while she took up his king-sized bed appealed to Nina's pettiness ... but not to the annoyingly devoted part of her that just wanted him comfortable and well-rested. Christ, that part was annoying.

She got up, heaving out a sigh, and pulled her pyjamas from her mammoth holdall. She'd spent the day hanging around at the garage because James refused to let her out of his sight, but now they were home and she was exhausted. She changed, grabbed her laptop, and wandered out into the living room. Returning to the scene of her greatest humiliation wasn't high on Nina's bucket list, but that was exactly why she had to do it. First of all, to show him that she didn't give a fuck. And second of all, to convince herself that, eventually, she *wouldn't* give a fuck.

She'd get over it. She would. The alternative was too depressing to think about.

She gritted her teeth and sat down on the innocuous-looking leather sofa, trying her best not to remember. It didn't work. The minute her arse touched the soft, dark cushions, her mind was assaulted by high-def, surround-sound recollections of That Moment. The picture-perfect slice of time when she'd really, actually believed that James wanted her. *All* of her. That she, the prickly freak who lived to bitch, the awkward, bullied emo, the big mouth who didn't know when to swallow her outrage or how to express her own pain, would get the guy.

She wasn't supposed to *want* to get the guy, but fuck that— love was important. Love was *good*. She loved James, and she'd wanted him to love her back.

He hadn't, of course. Not like that, anyway.

But she couldn't stop thinking about the blissful minutes when she'd believed he did. The way he'd stilled when she kissed him, just for a second, before wrapping his arms around her and kissing her right back. The way he'd touched her, so tender and reverent and barely restrained, as if underneath it all he was desperate. And the things he'd *said*—she'd never expected that from him, that flood of passionate honesty when they touched. He was always so calm, so steady, but when they'd been together ...

"God, Nina, I want you so much I can't breathe."

Her eyes slid shut.

And popped open again when she heard James's voice, not inside her head but from across the room.

"You hungry?"

Her cheeks burning, she turned to stare at him. He was standing in the doorway, looking good as fuck because he'd showered and changed. She liked his work clothes, but she liked regular James even better. He always dressed so well, as a kind of fuck-you to shops that didn't carry his size, so he was leaning against the doorframe in a mint shirt that made his brown skin shine, the sleeves rolled up to display the black line tattoos on his thick forearms. His soft grey trousers clung to his heavy thighs—but she really shouldn't be staring at his thighs. She shouldn't be staring at any of him, no matter how handsome he was.

Nina cleared her throat and opened up her laptop, patting nervously at her hair. Usually, she wouldn't care about the fact that her week-old braid-out was in need of a wash and refresh. Usually, she wouldn't think about James's handful of ex-girl-friends, most of whom he remained friends with, and all of whom were 24/7 gorgeous. She didn't compare herself to other women, ever. But right now she couldn't help wondering what he saw when he looked at her, and why it hadn't been enough.

Christ, what a gag-worthy thought.

"No," she said, working to keep her voice calm. "I'm fine, thanks."

There was a slight pause. He stared at her, his gaze a

burning spotlight on the side of her face. She kept her eyes on her laptop, the words on the bright screen blurring into nothing.

Finally, he said, "You're *not* hungry?"

"Nope," she repeated.

"You haven't eaten since that sub at lunch."

"I know what I've eaten, James."

He sighed. "Not to nag—"

"So don't."

"But if you don't get three square meals a day, you ..."

Despite herself, Nina felt a smile tug at her lips. She refused to give in to it. Still, her voice wasn't quite as dry as she'd like when she said, "I turn into a raging beast?"

"Not exactly how I was going to put it," he murmured, his amusement clear. He wandered closer, and for a moment it felt like old times, the two of them joking while he tried to look after her and she tried to resist. There was a slight teasing smile on his face, and laughter fought its way up her throat.

Maybe she shouldn't have stopped talking to him. It wasn't his fault that he didn't want her. She should've stayed calm, listened to his oh-so-considerate apology, and found a way to forgive him. Better yet, she never should've touched him in the first—

A word on the computer screen caught her attention with a jolt. She finally focused on the page in front of her, for real. And the tentative, wistful hope she'd been feeling was replaced by devastation.

James must've seen the blood drain from her face, because he frowned and came to kneel by her side. "What is it?"

"Nothing." She tried to shut the laptop, but his big hand caught hers. Giving her a warning look, he pushed the screen fully upright again. Together, they watched the constantly moving stream of posts.

@RealityCheckUK we got you now bitch

@RealityCheckUK gonna pay u a visit see how loud u scream

@RealityCheckUK this will teach you to look down on your betters you dumb ape

@RealityCheckUK—

James shut the laptop a little too hard and set it on the coffee table.

"Someone shared my address," she whispered, her blood cold and sluggish, creeping through her veins. "They know who I am."

"No," he said firmly. "They know you're from Nottingham. They *might* know where you live, but you're not there anymore. And we're handling it."

"The police won't do anything." Her lips were numb. "Not until it's too late. They never do. I knew a girl who ran a feminist sex blog—"

"Don't think about that," he cut in. "Don't think about any of it. And don't look at that shit anymore."

"Don't tell me what to do," she snapped, the words a reflex fuelled by fear.

If she'd meant to push him away, it didn't work. The opposite, in fact. Sweet-edged shock ripped through her as his hand cupped her cheek, the callouses on his palm rasping against her skin. He turned her face until they were eye to eye. "Nina. Love. Please don't look."

His familiar voice, low and rich and raw, felt like comfort. So did his touch. But he'd felt like comfort before, only for him to tear the connection away moments later. So she set her jaw and did the same, jerking away from his hold. "Alright. Fine. Whatever."

"Are you okay?"

God, why did he have to care about her? And why did she have to love him? Her voice hard, she clipped out, "Obviously."

"You want a hug?"

"I would honestly rather die."

"You're safe with me," he said, ignoring her completely. "You know I won't let anyone hurt you."

It was absolutely ridiculous, but it was also true.

God, she was a mess. She felt like she might fall apart at any moment. She *wanted* to fall apart, and James was the one person she could do it around, but not right now. Not with everything that lay between them.

He studied her for a moment, his gaze warm and sweet as hot chocolate. Then his hand caught hers. When she tried to pull away, he held on tight and shook his head. "We need to talk, Cupcake. Maybe now isn't the greatest time, but I already left things too long."

Oh, Christ. She felt as if her breath was too hot for her lungs. Embarrassment prickled across her skin. "James. Don't—"

"Nina. Please. Please let me try to fix this, because ..." He broke off, swallowing hard. "I can't lose you. And I feel like, if this nightmare hadn't happened, I might have."

She stared down at their joined hands, his fingers longer and thicker than hers, her skin darker and softer than his. She catalogued the little nicks and burns scattered across his knuckles and tried not to freak out. Tried not to hate him for speaking like this, speaking as if she meant the world to him, when things between them would never be the way she wanted.

"I'm sorry," he said. His thumb swept slow, rhythmic circles over the back of her hand, the action easing her tension even as his words ratcheted it up. "I fucked up. Massively. *Enormously.* Worse than whoever invented pop-up ads."

A smile crept onto her face without permission. "Continue."

He let out a little chuckle, shaking his head. Then his expression softened, becoming almost ... vulnerable. "Nina, when I was touching you, I couldn't think. I just couldn't. Which is ridiculous, and doesn't excuse my being irresponsible, but it's the truth. Then as soon as we were done, I just felt so *guilty*, and everything was flooding back into my brain at once, and it made me ... Well, I was thoughtless. I shouldn't have treated you like that. I'm sorry."

She nodded slowly. Parts of that speech soothed the jagged wound inside her, but others seemed to tear it open further. She wanted to sort sensibly through the two sensations, wanted to approach their issues in a calm, reasonable, mature way—but she wasn't calm, reasonable, or mature, so in the end she blurted out, "What the fuck, James?"

He blinked, running a hand over his jaw. "What?"

"I mean, okay, thank you. For the apology. But ... how were *you* irresponsible? What, exactly, did you feel guilty about?"

He opened and shut his mouth like a fish. A very handsome fish. A very *annoying* fish. Eventually, he said, "I told you. I shouldn't have done it."

She jerked back as if he'd hit her. "You mean you shouldn't have done *me*."

"That's not how I would put it, but ... No. I shouldn't have. We can't just—and then—like it doesn't even—" Yet again, James appeared to have been hit with the inarticulate stick. Apparently, sex was the one thing he could not talk fluently about. She might have found that funny, if she didn't suspect it came from his sheer embarrassment that he'd given in to his dick and slept with someone he didn't actually want.

"Nina," he said finally, "you're twenty-three years old."

"You didn't seem to mind that when you had your tongue between my legs."

He grimaced, letting go of her hand. "Sweetheart. Could you not—"

"What? Remind you of how awful it all was?"

24

"You know it wasn't awful." He stood, beginning to pace the room. Kind of annoying how the action that helped *him* focus made *her* want to throw something. "I hope I didn't ... Did it seem ...?" He hesitated, turning to frown at her. "Did I act like it was awful?"

She set her jaw, drawing her knees up to her chest and wishing, more than ever before, that she could just fucking disappear. "I mean, you threw me out half a second after finishing the job, so—"

"I did *not* throw you out," he said, his tone suddenly fierce. "I would never do that. You *left*."

"Okay, yeah. But you wanted me to leave."

"No I fucking didn't." He was speaking through gritted teeth now, his scowl ferocious. "I wanted to take back the whole thing—"

"Great! Fucking great!"

"But I never wanted you to leave."

"What's the bloody difference?"

"The difference is that no matter what happens between us, I *always* want you around. Always. Because you're way more important to me than sex or any of that bullshit. I mean, come on, Nina." He threw up his hands. "I know I said things all wrong, but I was right then and I'm right now. What are we going to do? Fuck each other and act like nothing happened? You want me to be like—" He broke off with a curse, turning away from her, and she knew he hadn't meant to say so much. Sometimes—very rarely—his temper got away from him. He hated it when that happened.

But even though she knew his mind must be a hurricane, she was too angry not to push. "Like what?" she demanded, rising to her feet. "Like me?"

"No," he said immediately, turning to look at her. "No. That's not what I meant."

She almost wanted to disbelieve him—to take his cut-off words as an insult, as a comment on her semi-notorious sex life. Some people in this city called her a man-eater. She truly did not give a fuck.

But if James had tried to hurt her like that, he'd have succeeded. And yet, she knew he hadn't, and never would.

"What, then?" she asked, wrapping her arms around herself. Tight. Tight enough to hurt, to push at her own ribcage.

"Stop that," he muttered, the words automatic, his tone distracted. He strode over and took hold of her wrists, tugging open her arms and sliding into the space he'd created. And now they were hugging, her cheek pressed to his shirt, his heartbeat strong under her ear, her tense muscles melting. Nina told those muscles, very sternly, not to bow to the enemy. She and James were having an argument, for fuck's sake. She should not be inhaling his scent like it was oxygen.

Still, she had the presence of mind to push again. "James?"

His hand came to rest at her nape, fingers sliding carefully into her hair. "Shh. I'm working up to something."

"To what?" She leaned back, trying to look at him, but he held her close.

"I'm putting my shit on the line here, Cupcake," he said wryly. "Give me a second."

"Stop calling me Cupcake."

"No. Mark and I swore a solemn vow to irritate you wherever possible, and I refuse to abandon my brother-in-arms."

She rolled her eyes. "Why, when I was born with only one older brother, have I been cursed with two?"

Abruptly, he pushed her back until their eyes met. His gaze was steady, even more serious than usual. "I'm not your brother, Nina. In any way. Trust me."

She felt an uncharacteristic blush heat her cheeks. "I know that. I—"

"I don't want you to think of me as a quick fuck," he said suddenly, the words cutting into the space between them. "That's why I stopped things, before. That's why I shouldn't have done it. You're young, and you're *you*, and I love you for it, but I can't be like these little boys you take to bed. We're not like that. We're friends. We matter."

Oh. *Oh.* Understanding was like a fist to the gut. It actually stole her breath, realising what had been going through his head. Did he really think she'd treat him like everyone else, treat him like those guys she ran through to take the edge off? She studied his face, one she knew as well as her own, and accepted that the answer was yes. He did.

He really had no idea what he meant to her. At all.

But what was she supposed to do? *Tell* him? Just ... admit her deepest, darkest secret, something that could blow up everything between them, from this fragile peace to the deepest foundations of their friendship? Fear clogged her throat at the thought. What would happen if she told him the truth? If she said, *I don't want to fuck you and act like nothing happened. I want you to be mine.*

Maybe he'd fall into her arms and confess his undying love. But, realistically, that wasn't the most likely outcome. Especially when he kept harping on about this whole friendship thing. Nina knew how to read between the lines, and James's were saying *I'm just not that into you.*

Maybe she should be brave and confess anyway. But she couldn't. She just couldn't. Even if she'd wanted to, her mouth wouldn't form the words. Everything was awful right now —*monumentally* awful—and this man was her only haven.

She couldn't risk it. She couldn't risk *him.*

Not now. Not ever.

So Nina took a deep breath and plastered a smile on her face. Nothing too huge, because that wouldn't be believable.

Just a tiny, wry twist of the lips, as if she were reluctantly agreeing with him. "Fair enough," she said softly. "You were right. We shouldn't have crossed the line."

His shoulders sagged. He gave a sigh that might have been relief. "Exactly. But we won't do it again."

Christ, did he have to sound so bloody emphatic? "No," she agreed.

"Okay. Good. Cool. So ..." He gave her a tentative smile. "Are you sure you're not hungry?"

"Actually," she murmured, "I'm starving."

Chapter Three

They were in the middle of some Marvel film or other, finished bowls of pasta on the coffee table and the sky outside growing dark, when Nina's nerves got the better of her.

She shouldn't have said anything. It was silly. It was weak. But the words tumbled out anyway, realer than they'd ever been.

"What if someone hurts me?"

There was a pause, in which Nina tried to psychologically kick herself—seriously, she could have used a steel-toed boot up the arse right now—and James presumably processed what she'd just said. She could feel his presence right beside her, the heat of their barely touching thighs, the creak of leather every time he shifted, the cadence of his steady breaths. So she sensed rather than saw him lean forward to pause the film.

Then he repeated his earlier words, his deep voice warm and comforting. "No one's hurting you, Cupcake. No one. I've got you."

The vulnerability she felt right now made her want to turn and hide—but that would be cowardly, wouldn't it? More cowardly than looking to him for the reassurance she needed, the reassurance he was so good at offering. So she turned toward him.

When their eyes met, his jaw shifted, as if he were struggling to hold in his words. But he didn't speak, and he didn't look away. In that moment she realised how often he *did* look away—how often James distracted himself around her, working on something as they talked. It was rare for them to sit in silence like this. To be so close, and so alone, like this.

It hadn't always been like that. When she was young—before her brother had left—James had been casually comfortable around her. Fond and unaffected. Then everything changed at once; she'd grown up, her brother had run off to feel like a part of something, and gradually, James had ... changed. In ways she couldn't name, had never thought to examine.

Maybe she'd consider all that later, when she could think without the solid weight of anxiety squeezing her brain.

"You're not a superhero," she told him flatly. "And you can't keep evil people under control through sheer force of will."

James seemed to flinch at the words, pressing his eyes shut for a breath. Then he opened them again, and suddenly his expression was so raw, so honest, it almost hurt to look at it. "If anyone touches you, I will kill them." He said it the way he said everything, quietly, steadily, certainly. She couldn't imagine James killing anyone. He was just ... *good*. Everything about him was good. But at that moment, for some reason, she believed him.

Maybe that should've scared her. Instead, it made her want to curl up in his lap like a cat and purr.

"I don't understand you," she admitted, the words squeezing at her own heart. She hated it, but it was true. Nina wanted to understand everything—that was why she'd started the website that got her into this mess. She'd wanted to understand the way this country worked, and when she'd figured it out, she'd wanted everyone else to know too.

Now she was an expert on EU subsidies and misleading rhetoric. She could tell you how many deaths had been caused by austerity so far, and she could recommend books that would explain the sociological biases that allowed those deaths to happen.

But she couldn't grasp why James was the way he was—how he could touch her so gently one minute and flinch away the next, how he could avoid her like the plague but swear he'd kill for her. And, truthfully, she couldn't fathom the depths of her own need for him, when her teenage crush had grown into something that felt molten and uncontrollable and painfully inevitable.

"What's there to understand?" he asked quietly. "You know I care about you."

"Because you love my brother."

"Because I love—" He broke off with a heavy sigh, shaking his head. "I'm sorry, Nina. Because if that's what you think, I haven't done right by you for a long time."

She eyed him warily. "What does that mean?"

"It means you're ... you're one of the most important people in my life, and you don't even know it. You should know it." He reached out and caught her hand, her nerve endings sparking like fireworks. Aside from their hug, this was the first solid touch she'd had from James in weeks, sitting on the sofa where he'd touched her, *really* touched her, for the last time. The quick flick of his whisky gaze, the tic of a muscle at his jaw were the only indications that he might be thinking the same. But within seconds his expression was smooth, his voice level and comforting.

Maybe she was imagining things.

"If I tell you something now," he said, "do you think you could try to believe me?"

She felt a smile tease her lips, despite the tumult of emotions in her chest. "*Something*, hm? We're not going to talk about our feelings, are we? Because you know how I feel about that."

"It's gotta happen sometime, Cupcake." James wasn't smiling back. He was deadly serious, his gaze insistent. He leaned toward her, and she was struck by the power of his body, the amount of space he took up. He was a big guy, which she liked, impressive muscles protected by a layer of sheer bulk. When he was sitting in front of her like this, in a thin white vest and basketball shorts, she was filled with the inappropriate urge to run her hands over his powerful body. To kiss the soft and vulnerable parts of him and luxuriate in the hard ones.

She cleared her throat and said, "I'll believe whatever you tell me. I know you're always honest."

It was true, but for some reason his expression darkened at the words. "Right. Right. Okay. Well ..." A moment ago he'd been calm and collected as ever, but now he seemed to be searching for words. "Well, first of all, I know we haven't seen each other in a while, but talking to you is the highlight of my day. I don't do it because of Mark. When he told me to look out for you, I don't think he meant 'Text her constantly'."

The rueful expression on his face made Nina smile. "We don't text *constantly*."

They texted constantly. Usually just dog pics, weird memes, and links to articles. But still.

James gave her a look and ignored the blatant lie. "Anyway. I also want you to know that, no matter how things are between us, I am never too busy for you. I pray that nothing like this ever happens again, but if it does, you need to know that. You need me, you call me. Fuck, you can call me if you break a fucking nail. I don't care, Nina. You need me, you call me. Because you matter. Okay?"

She looked away, trying not to choke on the emotions clogging her throat.

"Nina."

She grunted.

"*Nina.*" She registered the familiar exasperation in his voice, realised she was doing the whole emotional-distancing thing, seconds before he caught her by the wrist and pulled. The action sent her sprawling against his side, forcing her to lean on him when she felt more like wandering off.

"I think someone needs another hug, Cupcake," he said. She laughed automatically, because this was a familiar move—as familiar as the nickname itself. The whole thing had started as a joke between him and Mark.

"Damn, your little sister's a ray of sunshine."

"Oh, yeah. That's Nina: a marshmallow in human form."

"A walking, talking cupcake."

The punchline, of course, was her permanent scowl, pessimistic outlook, and love of the colour black.

But James always said it with such soul-deep fondness, she never felt like he was making fun of her. The moniker only annoyed her these days because it felt like a reminder to the both of them: *this can't happen. You're off-limits. You're my Cupcake.*

Well, he'd certainly eaten her like one. She glanced at him with a smirk. If James could read her mind, he'd probably spend most of his time in a horror-shock coma.

"What's so funny?" he demanded, and then, of course, he tickled her.

Nina's smile turned into an undignified snort, then a reluctant shriek. She rose up on her knees to escape; he pulled her close. She batted away his hands; he rolled his eyes and kept going. James was a lot bigger than she was, and singularly determined to make her laugh.

He succeeded, too—as always. Within seconds, she was breathless and giggling harder than she had in years. "Oh my God," she said finally, gasping for air. "Okay, okay, stop!"

He did, laughing himself, and for a moment, things were just like they used to be—back when Markus was around and James was just part of the furniture, like a second older brother with a hell of a lot more patience.

But as their laughter faded, so did the mirage of their memories. Because this wasn't before. Not even close. As this weird tension between them had grown, they'd lost the tactile element of their friendship. Every touch between them, once casual, now felt charged—at least it did to Nina.

And apparently to James too. They both seemed to realise at the same moment, with similar jolts of surprise, that she was practically sitting on his lap right now, having somehow managed to wiggle her way closer to his warmth. Christ, that was embarrassing. She saw the exact moment he noticed; the smile slid right off his face, replaced by an expression that was mostly uncertain, but partly something … darker. Something hot and secretive and guilty. The way his soft mouth hardened, the fire burning in his eyes, the tension in his muscles—it all reminded her of the way he'd looked when he'd settled between her thighs. On his knees. Worshipping her.

"Sorry," she mumbled, pushing the memory away. "Getting carried away with the old skin starvation. I, uh, I suppose I haven't touched anyone in a while."

"Why the hell not?"

His indignation was strong enough to draw an actual laugh from her. "I don't know. Would you like me to send out an email questionnaire?"

"No need," he said with a smile, wrapping his arms around

her. "Just stay here a second, would you?" He was looking at her again, all fond and soft and sweet and ... close. He had an amazing mouth. If he kissed her—

He's not going to kiss you.

But if he kissed her between her *legs*—

Okay! Time to excuse yourself and masturbate your way back to common sense.

Nina did not excuse herself. Instead, she put her head on his shoulder without thinking too hard about it. There was only the slightest pause, the slightest moment of tension, before he relaxed beneath her. He tightened his arms around her just enough, because James had always been a fan-fucking-tastic hugger.

They sat for a while, silent and still. She felt the rise and fall of his chest in time with his slow exhalations ghosting over her bare shoulder. She was ... peaceful, for a few minutes. Peaceful, and impressed with herself for holding off all impure thoughts despite their closeness. And his handsomeness. And the way he held her, and the scent of him, intoxicating as usual.

Then he shifted suddenly, pulling away. She was jolted back into full awareness, and when she looked up at his face, she found ...

Panic?

"Well," he said, his voice rougher than usual. "As long as you know." He looked over at the TV, seeming suddenly tense. "It's getting late. We should really get on with the film."

She blinked. "Are you okay?"

"Fine," he gritted out, rather unconvincingly.

"James, if—"

"I swear I'm fine, Cupcake. But we have a busy day tomorrow, so we should ..." He trailed off, which was baffling in itself. James wasn't really a mumble-y, stuttering sort of person. "Come on," he muttered, and then he *put his hands on her hips* and lifted her off him like she was a tissue. Which she most assuredly was not. Nina landed back on the sofa with an undignified plop, cheeks burning. What the hell was his problem? If he didn't want—

"I'm going to get some water," he blurted out, his words blurring together as he stood. Then he stalked out of the room like his arse was on fire, leaving Nina staring in confusion at the two full glasses on the coffee table.

Water.

He was going to get some water.

He was—

Oh. Gosh. Hm. Once upon a time, it would never have occurred to Nina that James Foster could be the victim of an accidental hard-on. But then, once upon a time, she'd never felt his tongue between her legs.

Well, now. This *was* interesting. And it certainly lessened the sting of their earlier *"I'm just not that into you"* conversation.

Of course, he still wasn't into her in the ways that mattered. But she refused to let that thought linger when she was already flirting with sadness 24/7. Positive vibes only. And here was a positive vibe: she made James horny whether he liked it or not. So there!

Nice to know she'd abandoned all dignity, even inside her own head, when it came to this particular man.

He returned ten minutes later, looking much more like himself, if a little brisk. "You want to play the film?" he asked quickly, like if he spoke first, she might not ask any awkward questions. When he sat down, squashing himself into the corner of the sofa, he managed to leave an acre of space between them.

Nina bit back a smile. "Sure. You know how much I love men in skintight outfits, even if they are subtle advocates of eugenics and a militarised form of vigilante 'justice'."

"Oh, for God's sake," James snorted, his full lips curving into a smile.

"Hey, you asked."

The look he gave her was warm, almost unbearably so. "I did, didn't I?"

He pressed play.

Chapter Four

"Nina, sweetheart, you're so fucking wet." James sucked on her swollen clit and explored her glossy folds with his fingertips. When she arched toward him and moaned in response, satisfaction hit him like a bolt of lightning. He was good at this. He was good at her. Which made sense. When you knew a woman this well and watched her this close and cared this fucking much, it added up.

"Let me taste you," he murmured, his voice so low he could barely hear himself. "I need to taste you." He licked lower, savoured the tang of her honey, pressed his hard dick into the sofa cushions and rubbed his cheek against her inner thigh. Nina's inner thigh. How the hell did he get here, at the apex of his fucking fantasies?

James had been so confused when she kissed him, but the confusion hadn't lasted long. Knowing he shouldn't think about her like this, shoving away the instinct to look too closely, pretending he didn't see her face every time he touched himself —those things were easy. But when Nina came over and kissed him, when she slipped that soft, sweet tongue into his mouth and pressed her little tits against his chest and said his name ...

That had been hard.

James was so fucking hard.

But he shouldn't be doing this. He should stop right now. He should—

James woke up with a jolt and promptly fell right off the sofa. Jesus fucking Christ. His hip made sharp contact with the floor, his elbow knocked into the coffee table, but he barely felt it. His chest heaved with each laboured breath, his blood pulsed hard enough to fizz and ache beneath his skin, and his cock ...

His cock was rigid and straining for release, his own pre-come seeping steadily and stickily against his stomach. He rushed out a sigh and licked his lips, desperate to chase away the phantom taste of Nina on his tongue. The slightly salty bite and deep, drugging perfume of her wet pussy. So wrong. And such a bad fucking idea. But God—he pressed a fist to his mouth, biting down to stifle a groan. His dick fucking *hurt.*

James heaved himself back up onto the sofa, the same one his Nina had writhed on as she came. But no, not *his*, she couldn't be his—she'd only felt that way, for a moment. Lying there, those sharp eyes soft with the pleasure he gave her, her pussy spread open like a honey-dipped bloom, begging for his tongue, his fingers ... Oh yeah. She'd felt like his then.

You should've given her your cock when you had the chance. She'd take it so sweetly.

And now she was just down the hall, in James's bed, all alone. If he went to her ...

But no. He couldn't. He mustn't. Aside from all the reasons why it would be wrong—he looked out for her, she needed him, he was literally responsible for her protection now—Nina simply didn't want the things James wanted. Didn't want the romance, the commitment, the intimate connection he craved with her and her alone. And he couldn't take anything less. Not ever, but certainly not with her.

Knowing all of that didn't do his erection any good, though. His cock was still pointing up at him accusingly, like it blamed him personally for the current lack of Nina's pussy around it.

With a helpless groan, James gave up a little of his hard-won control. Ignoring his better instincts, he shoved down his briefs and fisted his own length.

So. Fucking. Good.

A moan caught in his throat as he squeezed himself, as sweet pressure offered a hint of relief.

"Please. James. Touch me."

His hand was bigger, harder, rougher than Nina's, but he closed his fucking eyes and imagined.

Imagined her tight grip stroking him, teasing him, milking the come from his heavy, desperate balls.

Imagined her sweet, filthy mouth pressing kisses over his fevered skin.

Imagined her whispering his name, that she wanted him, only him, *because* it was him ...

And then he heard her. For real.

A soft little gasp, one that had been seared into his memory weeks ago alongside the taste of her pussy, one he'd recognise anywhere.

His eyes snapped open, and there she stood in the moonlit shadows of the room. Nina. She wore a white top that displayed her stiff nipples like rock-hard diamonds, and tight lacy knickers that clung to the plump curve of her mound. Her eyes were wide, and her mouth was a lush O of shock. He blinked, but she didn't go away.

Nina was really standing right there.

And for Christ's sake, she looked like a dream, like a fuck fantasy. James knew he should put his dick away and start making excuses but ...

Clearly, he was delirious with exhaustion or with plain

old lust, because instead of horror, all he felt was the tingling at the base of his spine that meant he'd be coming sooner rather than later. Something must have possessed him, because all he could do was hold her midnight gaze and keep jerking himself.

And Nina didn't move. Didn't look away. Didn't make a sound. Just watched him, looking as hungry—as *starving* for this —as James felt.

He couldn't stop imagining how he might use that still-open mouth, how he might worship the cunt her underwear clung to. Her gaze dropped to his lap—to his thick, hard cock, standing crudely between them like a neon sign. Her eyelids drooped, her chest rising and falling as her breaths stuttered. He heard his own heartbeat in his ears.

And then one of Nina's delicate little hands crept down over her hips and slipped beneath the waistband of her underwear. James swore he almost passed the fuck out. She caught his gaze again, held it, and he understood the message hidden there.

Just this once.

He felt it too, a whisper shivering through his blood, like a secret sent directly from his heart. But that couldn't be right, because *"just this once"* with Nina was guaranteed to rip the heart from his chest.

Really? You seriously can't just come and get over it, Foster?

Not with her. Especially not after their conversation this evening, when he'd asked her—begged her—to say that he was different, that *they* were different ... and she hadn't.

Because they weren't.

But God, he was really fucking horny, and she must be too, because her hand delved deeper. He could see the outline of her fingers through thin white fabric as she parted her own pussy lips. Her head fell back, exposing the long, elegant line of her neck as she moaned.

Talia Hibbert

Fuck. *Fuck.* If Nina needed this, who was he to take it away?

Resist her.

Protect her.

Give her what she needs.

James felt his hand flex on his cock and knew what he'd do before he'd consciously made the choice. He managed to force out a few words, his voice rasping between them in the dark. "You stay over there. I stay over here. When you're done, Nina, go to sleep."

She looked at him, something he couldn't quite identify flashing in her gaze. "And then tomorrow we pretend nothing happened?"

He tightened his jaw.

"Alright, James," she murmured, a slight ironic smile curving her lips. "It was just a dream." He heard something in her words that he wanted to follow, to investigate, to expose—but then she leaned back against the wall and eased off her underwear, shimmying it down to the floor and kicking it away. She raised one knee, pressing her foot flat to the wall behind her. The hint of her cunt he saw in the barely-there light was enough to make James wild with need, and his memory filled in the rest: her parted lips. That swollen clit. The honeyed taste of her.

He choked out a moan and stroked his cock faster and harder, determined to make himself mindless. If he couldn't resist, not tonight, then he might as well fucking enjoy.

And beat himself up for it later.

Nina arched her back, pushing her hips forward as she trailed delicate fingers around her swollen nub. He knew just how she liked to be sucked, how she begged and sobbed for his tongue to lave her there. Now, without him, she massaged herself with two fingers, slow and firm. He imagined his tongue

42

doing that for her. Imagined her getting wetter against his beard. Then he all but throttled his own dick.

She brought down her other hand and, without preamble, pushed three fingers into her pussy.

"Fuuuck." The word was low and tight, rushing from James's throat without permission. "Oh, my God ..." He couldn't bring himself to say her name again, to make this moment real. But inside his mind, he chanted *Nina, Nina, Nina* as he watched her fuck herself. "Are you that wet, baby? Do you need it that bad?" He shouldn't be asking her this, shouldn't be talking to her at all. But he'd been right—she'd take his cock so fucking sweet, and never mind his size. She'd beg for it and writhe on it and love it. He should ask her. He should tell her. He should get up and fucking *give* it to her.

No. No. *No.*

Maybe later he'd come to his senses and realise that fairy-tale logic about not touching the princess or speaking her name didn't make a damn difference in the real world—that he'd fucked Nina from halfway across the room just as truly as if he'd put his dick inside her. But right now ...

Right now, nothing was tearing him away from this.

"Yeah," she moaned, spreading her legs wider, fucking herself deeper, rubbing her clit with almost frantic intensity. "Yeah, I need it. God, James."

At the sound of his name on her lips, his cock jumped, and he felt a hot spurt of come against his belly.

"You look so fucking gorgeous," Nina whispered into the silence. "I'm going to come so fast—"

James groaned and gave up fighting his own release. He embarrassed himself with his own orgasm, it was so long and so hard. He saw black, he saw stars, he saw *Nina*. He came all over himself, and it was so fucking satisfying he could barely regret it.

He opened his eyes in time to see Nina coming too, and he certainly didn't regret *that*. Her moans were short, sharp little things that rose to a crescendo, her body shuddering, her fingers still working that greedy little pussy. "James," she whispered, just for him, and the sound of it was a drug.

He'd never stood a fucking chance.

Chapter Five

"We've created an incident, Ms. Chapman," the strawberry-blonde copper droned. Airey, he'd said his name was—not that James cared. The man had spent the last half hour asking Nina pointless questions that verged on rude and scribbling down her answers with a sceptical air. "Someone will be in touch about any further developments."

James had kept his mouth shut throughout the whole infuriating morning, but he wasn't a fucking saint. He couldn't let a complete dismissal slide. *"Any further developments?"* he echoed, incredulous. "This is an active threat. She was doxed yesterday, regardless of the fact they got the wrong address. They know where she's from. She's receiving hate right now."

The officer arched one pale brow, as if James had spoken nonsense instead of laying out facts. "Ms. Chapman has made it clear that, upon investigation, the address shared as hers was incorrect. *Therefore*, she was not doxed. We can't just click our fingers and stop online harassment. There are procedures to be followed. In the meantime, have you tried blocking the perpetrators?"

James stared. "Have we tried. Blocking. The people. Who send. Death threats?"

Nina's hand came to rest on his arm. "James—"

"Are you serious? That's a question you're seriously asking?"

The policeman's expression hardened. "Please mind your tone when you speak to me, *sir*."

James gritted his teeth and ignored the sly inflection. "A young woman comes in here fearing for her life, and you talk to her like a robot. No reassurances, no concern for her safety, nothing but taking notes and handing out incident numbers. And you want to talk about *my* tone?"

"James, that's enough." Nina shot to her feet, her chair scraping against the floor with a sound that rattled through the station. "I'm sorry, PC Airey. Thank you very much for your time."

James took a deep breath, closed his eyes for the barest second—just long enough to regain his control. He seemed incapable of holding it for long when it came to this woman. But he had to try.

Especially after failing so epically last night.

"Right," he said, standing up. "Apologies." If the word sounded more like a knife than a genuine statement, that couldn't be helped. What a load of bastards.

He caught Nina's hand, though he wasn't sure why—to comfort her, or to soothe himself? Maybe both. It was odd that her touch should still calm him, when in certain contexts it could drive him out of his mind, but he'd learned that that sort of duality was part and parcel of being in love with her. Today, he'd learned another aspect of being in love with Nina: it meant that he lost his fucking temper when people looked down on her. Lost his temper, as in, briefly considered throwing a chair at a police officer's head.

"Well," he burst out as they left the building. "That was a waste of time."

"Told you," she said mildly. She hadn't let go of his hand. She was swinging it gently, like they were children, and the Nina Neuroses that ran constantly in the background of his mind wanted to know *does that mean she's forgotten all about the other night? Is she really unaffected? Does sex really mean— no, does sex with me really mean nothing to her? And why am I wondering about this when I already know the answer, and why the hell did I—*

He turned away from the voice. Considering his current fury, it wasn't hard. "They didn't even care."

"I know."

"And why the fuck did they keep bringing up your record?" He rubbed a free hand over his beard and scowled at the police force logo imprinted into the paving stones in front of them. "What possible relevance could that have?"

"James—"

"It's not like you're a fucking murderer! It's not like you run around assaulting old ladies! So you tied yourself to a few trees—"

"James."

"So you obstructed some traffic—"

"James! You're shouting."

"I ..." He came back to himself, feeling as surprised as Nina looked by his outburst. Slowly, James looked around to discover that they were still standing in front of the police station, passers-by gawking at him. As he made eye contact with each one, the watchers shook themselves and hurried off about their business. Which, considering James's present mood, was probably wise of them.

"Come on," Nina said firmly. She tightened her grip on his hand, dragging him down the street until they came to the area's little park. Daffodils stood to attention in cheerful clumps about the grass, and children played on the climbing frame metres away. James took a breath of spring-scented air and let Nina shove him onto a bench.

"Now," she said, plonking herself beside him. "Do we really need to have a conversation about why you should not lose your temper in a police station, James?"

He sighed. "No."

"Would you like to explain why you recklessly put yourself at risk over my feelings?"

Because your feelings mean the world, he managed not to say. "I didn't think."

"Clearly fucking not. Do you see yourself? Better yet, do you know how *they* see you?"

"Yes."

"*As a threat*," she snapped, as if he hadn't spoken.

He turned to face her. "Nina. Sweetheart. I'm sorry."

She nodded stiffly. He heard her swallow.

"I'm sorry," he repeated. "I'm sorry. Come here."

She let him pull her closer—maybe a little too close, with her thigh pressed against his, and his arm around her shoulders. But fuck it. Now they were sitting like this, he could feel her shaking. She needed him.

He needed her, too.

James sat back against the bench, holding her tight, and watched the birds hop across the dewy grass. When Nina snuggled into him, her hand resting against his belly, he told himself that she was seeking shelter from the cool morning breeze. That was all.

He'd had a moment of wild hope yesterday, when they'd talked about that first, forbidden time between them. He'd thought that she might hear the subtext in his awkward speech and tell him that it was okay, that things between them were different, that being with him had meant something.

But she hadn't said any of those things, because she wasn't a liar.

He swallowed his disappointment for what felt like the thousandth time and tried to enjoy what he had. Nina. Her friendship. Her presence.

The memories of her moaning for you last night.

No. Not that. That was off-limits if he wanted to maintain his sanity.

As if she sensed his disquiet, Nina straightened with sudden energy, narrowing her eyes in his direction. "You know what we need?"

James was instantly wary. "No. But I do know that when you get that look on your face, it never ends well for me."

She laughed, alight with a determination he unfortunately recognised, a determination that meant she was plotting. "Come on," she said, and then she dragged him to his feet.

———

"You cannot be serious."

"Oh, but I can," Nina sang, a wicked smile tilting her lips. James really could've done without that smile right now; he was still furious at the shitty police response, and he was incredulous at where Nina had brought him. Add *"reluctant lust"* to the list of his current emotions and he was in danger of getting a headache.

And, much to his shame, a dick-ache. Because Nina had smiled like that on the day he'd gotten between her thighs, lips curving in pleasure before his tongue slipped inside her and that mouth of hers parted on a filthy moan ...

"James?" She patted his arm. "You okay?"

Shit.

Focus, Foster—on something other than the memory of how good her pussy tastes.

"I'm just trying not to stroke out over the fact that you've brought me to Bounce Nation," he scoffed, scowling at his surroundings with a renewed sense of alarm. The children's amusement centre was located on the top floor of what used to be a lace factory. The brick walls and high ceilings were now splashed in purple and grey alien decor, with netted-off sections of wall-to-floor trampolines and bouncy castles placed all around. On the far side of the room was a concession stand selling radioactive-looking Slush Puppies and rubbery hotdogs. Screaming siblings and balloon-waving birthday parties surrounded them in the queue for Bounce Nation wristbands, all of which at least made for a solid distraction from impure thoughts.

"Trust me," Nina said sternly as she tugged him forward in the line. "This is gonna be great."

"This place is for children, Cupcake," he muttered, throwing furtive glances around. Could any of these kid-corralling women tell he was lusting after his best friend's little sister right now? Probably. Mums always knew things. In a second, they'd all start edging away from him like he was radioactive.

"Actually, there's an adults-only section," Nina informed him with a pert little grin. "Apparently it's great cardio."

"Oh, because we love cardio."

She stuck her tongue out. "Speak for yourself, James Foster. I'll have you know I occasionally walk to places, sometimes."

The unselfconscious pleasure on her face, so rarely seen these days, was mildly hypnotic. James found himself torn between capturing it like the precious thing it was, and letting it soar unhindered like a shooting star. Maybe making a fool of himself on a children's trampoline wouldn't be so bad, if it kept Nina in this good a mood.

He wasn't entirely confident that these things, "adult section" or not, would hold his weight when bouncing around, but … "Would this make you happy, Cupcake?"

She rolled her eyes, but her smile didn't fade. "I think it would make both of us *happier*. Endorphins and whatnot. That's the point."

For such a prickly little thing, she sure did seem to care about his moods. "Fine," he said. "Let's do it."

Her eyes lit up, and he was ruined.

"I don't trust this," James said in an adorably grumpy tone of voice. A frown creased his brow as he jabbed a foot onto the empty trampoline platform of the adult section. Nina rolled her eyes, forced her thoughts away from the plump curve of his arse in those dove-grey trousers, and rushed past him onto the trampoline.

"Come on," she ordered, sounding militant even to her own ears. "You promised me fun. We will have fun."

His expression softened into familiar exasperation. "Alright, Cupcake," he snorted. "Keep your hair on."

Brattiness always worked with James. Perhaps she should try pouting a little the next time she caught him with his dick out, and he might touch her or kiss her or say her name or—

No, no, no. There would not *be* a next time, because she had made the mature and adult decision to practise the fine art of staying her arse in bed for as long as she lived under James's roof. The other night had been …

Well.

But it couldn't be repeated.

51

Her heart was about as bruised as her pussy was satisfied. Because she couldn't forget that James didn't really want her— not properly. Not in the daylight, not in his right mind. There was no use letting that fact sting. She just had to be a grown-up about it and stop leaning into the blade.

But damn, he made it so hard.

James was biting his lower lip in concentration as he strode —yes, strode, with impressive balance—onto the springy plat- form, his expression as suspicious as his steps were aggressive.

"I don't think you can dominate the trampoline, James," she called over the sound of her own tentative bounces.

He looked up at her, dark eyes gleaming as he arched a wicked eyebrow. "Can't I?"

And God, that gravel voice and that solid jaw, and his shirt sleeves rolled up to expose those thick, tattooed forearms of his ... She was dizzy. She was absolutely dizzy. She moved forward, everything about him hooking into her and dragging her closer. He was so goddamn sweet, this man, doing whatever it took to calm and entertain her. Ever since they'd discovered that the address shared as Nina's ... wasn't, she'd wondered if his protection might disappear, or at best, fade away. Clearly, she wasn't in as much danger as they'd worried. But she *was* still anxious as hell—and without her ever saying so, James had done all it took to support her and keep her steady.

Maybe that was why he'd let them cross the line again last night. Maybe he could tell she needed it. After all, James was protective enough to take his *look-after-Nina* mission really, really far.

She should probably be upset by that idea—that they'd essentially had pity sex. Or therapy sex. Or something like that. But whenever she thought about it, all she could focus on was how horrifically hot he'd looked, sprawled naked on that sofa like a huge, lusty god, his dick so thick and hard in his hand.

He was just as handsome now, too, even fully clothed. Watching her with a fading smile, awareness creeping into his gaze, resistance written in the curl of his fists and the regretful curve of his mouth.

Ah, that mouth. Gorgeous and infuriatingly responsible and so determined to reject her.

"Nina," he said softly as she approached.

She didn't need him to finish that sentence. *Nina, don't.*

Shoving her clearly unwanted feelings away, she pasted on a smile—as if she could will away this electric tension by wanting it enough. James certainly seemed to think that was possible. "Alright. Time to stop stalling. Let's do this," she said, and then she bounced as hard as she possibly could.

Big mistake.

Nina wasn't blessed in the boob department—hers could best be described as *"modest"*. But it became instantly clear that her everyday bralette wasn't sturdy enough for Tits on Tour: Bounce Nation Edition. She triggered an earthquake-level boob rebound, instinctively grabbed them with both hands, then yelped and swung mortified eyes to James.

Who was doubled over with laughter, his section of trampoline shaking beneath him.

Just like that, Nina found herself grinning—even as she gasped with mock outrage, "Are you *laughing* at my pain, sir?"

Which only made him laugh harder. In fact, for a moment, she was worried he might be having some sort of fit. "Jesus Christ," he finally said. "You looked so fucking surprised, anyone would think you'd borrowed that chest for the weekend."

"I didn't think!" she protested.

"Clearly!"

"Stop laughing. For all you know, I'm suffering with frightful boob bruising as we speak."

Predictably, James's laughter dissolved into a concerned frown. He looked her up and down as if his eyeballs were capable of MRI scans. "Well, are you?"

"No," she admitted, "but I think I'll have to, er, hold on to these if I'm going to have any fun today." She gave her boobs an awkward shake, as if he might have forgotten their topic of discussion some time in the last five seconds.

"Fine," James said, and for one delicious moment she could have sworn that, beneath the calmness of the word, he was blushing. "Hold on to your tits, then."

"Said the vicar to the—argh!" Nina broke off as James burst into movement, jumping next to her with enough force to send her flying halfway across the space.

She landed on her arse a few metres away, bouncing, bouncing, bouncing until she came to a gradual stop.

At which point, her pulse racing, all the stress of the past weeks melting away, she grinned wide. And said just one word.

"*Again.*"

James smiled back at her. "And here I worried you hadn't thought the whole 'giant James' thing through."

"You should know by now," she said as she rose to her feet, "that nothing about you is too big for me."

"Nina." He rolled his eyes, refusing to take the bait.

Didn't matter. This wasn't just a tease; it was the truth. "You, James Foster," she murmured to herself, "are just right."

Chapter Six

On their way out of Bounce Nation, they bumped into a harried-looking father and a gaggle of sugar-high kids at the door. Nina's arm brushed James's as they stepped aside, and something electric crackled over the surface of his skin.

For fuck's sake. This was getting ridiculous.

"Admit it," she sing-songed as they stepped out onto the street. Evening had fallen, and this back road was quieter than it had been hours ago.

Jesus, had they really arrived hours ago?

"Admit what, Cupcake?"

"I was right. It was fun. And you loved it." She ticked off each item on her fingers with obvious glee. Nina always had loved to be right. And James had come to find satisfaction very attractive in a woman.

"Yeah," he sighed. "You were right. That was a surprisingly good stress-reliever." But the grin he couldn't wipe off his face had nothing to do with Bounce Nation and everything to do with how Nina looked in this moment: young, carefree, smiling wide with her pretty eyes crinkled at the corners. God, he wanted to kiss her.

Wanted it too much, apparently, because he found his steps slowing as he stared down at that lush mouth. A sudden silence blossomed between them, Nina's smile fading as she bit her lip. Around them, the city sank steadily into darkness, and the orange tinge of the street lights bounced off her thick, dark curls. He imagined bending just enough to drag his mouth over her smooth skin. Imagined kissing her cheek, her jaw, her throat. Grabbing a fistful of her hair to keep her still, feeling the curves beneath her huge black T-shirt when she pressed against him.

Last night, James had convinced himself he could have another taste of her, from a distance this time, and continue with business as usual. He could only blame such a major miscalculation on the fact that his brain had been starved of oxygen at the time, on account of all his blood going to his dick. Because the reality was this: every time he grew closer to Nina, every time he touched her or saw her or experienced her in some new way, she became more and more impossible to forget.

Remember why you can't have her.

He started checking off each item on the list. They wanted different things. He couldn't risk their friendship. She had more important stuff to think about right now. He'd known her when she was young, and he still couldn't decide if his attraction to her was kind of creepy for that reason.

But then she whispered, "James," so sweetly, as if his was the only name she'd ever bother to speak again, and common sense fell right out of his head. His heart shuddered. His blood pulsed. His hands flexed at his sides with the need to hold her.

He had to do something about this.

"Remind me," he said through clenched teeth.

"What?" Nina seemed to be floating toward him—or maybe he was moving toward her. Maybe the air between them was just fucking shrinking. James didn't know. He was sure of only two things right now.

That touching this woman would soothe something in him no one else could.

And that he absolutely could not let that happen.

James had the unnerving feeling that somewhere in him lurked a beast only Nina could release, one that would never let her go.

"Remind me," he said again. "What was it you used to tell Markus and me? About men?"

He watched as confusion furrowed her brow, then turned into realisation—and something else, something he couldn't quite identify.

Slowly, her lips tipped into a one-sided smile, and she repeated her own teenage mantra. "Mine for a good time, not for a long time."

James breathed the familiar words in and exhaled a new, hardened resolve. This was what it meant to be with Nina: to be temporary. He knew it, and he loved her just as she was, but he still had to protect his devoted, possessive heart at all costs. Maybe she'd have him again, and again, and again—but eventually, she'd be done. She'd walk away with no attachments, while he might be in danger of tattooing her name on his arse, or something equally disturbing. And James really didn't want to be that guy.

His jaw hard, he nodded and turned in the direction of home, but a soft hand on his forearm brought him up short. He looked at Nina again and found her expression serious.

"James, why did you want to know that?"

He forced a smile. "It just came to me. The memory, I mean. Couldn't quite remember the wording. It was funny."

"It was years ago," she shot back, "and it would be irrelevant if ... if I—" She pressed her lips tightly together, looking vaguely tortured, and James realised she was about to say something involving emotions and feelings and all the other shit she usually found so abhorrent.

"James," she started again, "you don't think that—"

A voice carved through the closeness of their conversation, rising above the rumble of passing cars. "Oi! That's her, I swear that's her. Are you that Brexit girl?"

James stiffened. In an instant, everything inside him—the need, the resignation, the careful, barely restrained yearning—sharpened to a fine pinpoint. It was the knife's edge of a blade named violence.

He forgot his feelings, forgot their conversation, forgot everything he had ever known except for three basic facts. Nina's position beside him. The position of the three men up the street, the men standing and staring and shouting at Nina, drunk off each other's presence in that way weak, dangerous men often were. And finally, James remembered everything he'd ever learned during decades of competitive kickboxing, lessons stamped into his bones through blood, sweat and tears.

As the men approached, a prowling pack of hyenas, he shoved Nina behind him and ordered tightly, "Do *not* move."

"James—"

"Nina, listen to me. Do. Not. Move."

He heard her shaky intake of breath, felt the press of her palm against his back. Knew that for once, she would listen. Reassured, he zeroed in on the approaching men again.

When they were a few metres away, he folded his arms and asked steadily, "Do we have a problem, gentlemen?"

The group, who had slowed down noticeably when Nina disappeared behind James, now came to a stop. The de facto leader, a scrawny white guy in a crumpled polo shirt and chinos, shot James a wary look. He shrugged, then looked back at his mates as if to remind himself of their presence, before stepping forward to reply. "No problem, pal," he said. "Just thought we saw ... someone."

"Well," James said evenly, "you didn't. So turn around and piss off."

Henchman number one, to the left of their fearless leader, hardened his rat-like jaw and adjusted the cap on his pin-head. "Alright, mate, calm down. Thing is, yeah, this is a free fucking country. No one's telling me what to do. Not you"—he spat on the ground—"or *her*."

Fury racing through James's blood, he surged forward. "This is the last time I repeat myself. Turn. The fuck. Around." He looked at each man in turn, holding their gazes, letting them see.

See everything feral in him, just ready and waiting to come to the fore.

Maybe it was his size, the sight of his clenched fists, or something else, something vicious vibrating through his bones. Whatever the case, the leader caught his friend's arm in an iron grip and muttered, "Come on, Harry. Ain't worth the fucking mess." They turned and left, their shadows receding around the corner until the street was empty but for passing cars again.

When James was certain they were gone, and his adrenaline had faded enough for him to do more than growl, he spun around and dragged Nina into his arms. She grabbed him right back, burrowing against his chest, grasping fistfuls of his jumper. Her hair tickled his jaw, her breaths coming quick against the hollow at the base of his throat. She smelled like coconut oil and sweat and unexpected, unnerving trust.

For a moment—just a second—James let himself forget that there were certain things he shouldn't feel. Desperate affection flooded his senses until he was almost weak with it. He might be twice Nina's size, but right now it felt like she was the one holding him up.

Protect her. You have to protect her.

Always.

Sometimes he felt as if he'd been made for it.

"I didn't …" Her usually strident voice was tentative, fragile as spun sugar. "I didn't expect … I knew people were saying things online, but I don't think I *really* believed they'd …"

Recognise her? Approach her? Make it real?

Despite what she'd already been through, with the doxing, the threats, the swarm of right-wing journalists who'd rushed to expose Nina's views to their massive followings … James clearly hadn't believed this would become real either. Because the shock he felt right now was just too visceral.

But it all made a sick sort of sense. This political minefield had hooked its claws under the skin of so many citizens, and they were letting it drag them around like puppets. The widespread frenzy loosened tongues and inhibitions, bringing to light all the little violences people had once hidden. There was something sour at the root of this nation, a bitter evil that had been buried rather than exposed and healed. Some political issues excelled in dragging that bitterness to the fore.

Nina knew all this, so James didn't piss her off by trying to explain it. He just held her tighter and whispered, "Shh. I've got you. It was bad luck. This is a small city. But this moment, all this attention, it will fade." He swallowed. "And I'll always be here. As long as you need me."

He meant it. Which was yet another reason to resist her, to resist his own desire. James could never leave Nina again, regardless of whether or not this nightmare blew over. He understood that now. So, to stay by her side, he had to remain steady. Reliable. Permanent.

He couldn't complicate matters between them. He couldn't become temporary.

Maybe it wouldn't have to be like that, whispered a hopeful voice at the back of his mind. Nina's a smart woman. Explain to her, calmly and logically, that she's yours, and if she agrees with your reasoning she might just let it happen.

James shook his head and decided he was still high on adrenaline. He turned his focus back to scouting their surroundings while stroking Nina's hair.

Long moments passed before she stirred. After several deep breaths, she pushed back slightly, looking up at him. There was steel in her dark gaze, her jaw, her spine. She was defiant again, determined again.

Just like that.

God, he loved this woman.

"I think you were right, before," she said, her voice utterly steady.

James arched an eyebrow. "About what?"

"Help. I need more of it." She took out her phone.

Chapter Seven

They went home, stuffed their faces with pizza, and watched old Syfy reruns where the bad guys got stabbed or thrown into the centre of the sun or brainwashed with green goo every time. James watched Nina closely, noticed her sending furtive texts and staring into space with what he called her "thinking face" firmly in place. He worried and hoped in equal measures. Worried because earlier tonight, Nina had been scared, and he hated the rare sight of Nina scared.

Hoped because Nina was also brilliant. Her mind and her mean streak were both wicked-sharp—especially when provoked.

When bedtime rolled around, they slipped easily into a routine: cleaning the kitchen, sharing the bathroom, Nina humming as she brushed her teeth, James trying not to get attached to the domestic feel of it all.

He bid her goodnight, turned all the lights off, and checked his phone. There was an email from Markus. James winced, imagining how a conversation between them would go right now, if he had the balls to be honest.

Hey, man. You know how you asked me, last Christmas, if I

was into your sister, and I laughed my arse off and asked you how the hell that would've happened? I lied. Sorry. Stay safe, by the way.

He left the email unopened.

Sleep was fitful, when it came, but he'd expected that. He wasn't surprised when thoughts of Nina—protecting her, holding her, *having* her—kept him awake and restless on the squashed-up little sofa.

And he wasn't shocked to find his hand sliding down to his hard cock again in the very early hours of the morning.

But somehow when Nina appeared in the doorway like a dream, like a wish, like a fantasy he didn't deserve to taste—that was what knocked him on his arse.

He stared at her for a moment in the near darkness, like she might disappear if he waited long enough. But maybe this made sense. She'd been scared. She'd needed him. And she needed him still.

Send her away. Three times is a pattern. We can't be a pattern.

But fuck, she looked so small and so alone, standing by the window. James sat up, swallowing hard as he took in the curls piled on top of her head, the eyes free of makeup and more vulnerable for it, the nervous slide of her hands over her bare thighs.

Although he must have that part wrong, somehow. Nina couldn't actually be nervous. Nina was never nervous, and she had no reason to be that way with him. Did she?

The question nagged at him, set him on edge. Maybe that was why, when he meant to tell her to leave, he accidentally said, "Come here."

She was standing in front of him in seconds, her body slotting into the space between his open knees like she belonged there. For a moment he couldn't even see her scantily clad body

—the shadow of her mound or the curve of her belly or the stiff tips of her nipples through her top—because he was way too focused on her face. Her beautiful, familiar face, the one that had been stamped with fear earlier and now looked just a little tense.

Maybe if he touched her now, he'd be taking care of her. Maybe saying no would make a bad night worse. Maybe this was actually his moral duty. James told himself all these bullshit things over the pounding of his pulse, and pretended he believed them.

"You okay, sweetheart?" he whispered.

Nina shrugged, which, as far as James was concerned, meant *no*. Then she put her hands on his shoulders, leaning on him slightly—which, as far as James was concerned, meant *help me*.

All he could think was, Yes, ma'am.

He ran his hands over her thighs, her hips, then round to squeeze the swell of her arse. She released a soft little sound and let her head fall back. A hunger for more of her reactions roared to life in him, and he bent forward to brush a kiss against her skin. His mouth met the tender strip of stomach between her top and her underwear. She shivered, moaned, urged him on with every restless shift and wordless sigh of pleasure.

Yes, yes, yes.

James opened his mouth, introduced the tip of his tongue to those slow, sucking kisses. Pushed her top higher and higher, his lips following, until she was panting hard enough for him to hear over the rush of blood in his ears. When he kissed the underside of her breast, she moaned, "Fuck, James," and the words acted like lightning in his blood. He was on fire, electrified. Loving this woman had never felt more urgent.

He pulled her down until she was straddling him, then peeled off her top completely, leaving her in nothing but her knickers, bare-chested and blushless in his lap. She cupped the back of his head with shaking hands and arched toward him. "Please," she whispered.

"So pretty when you beg, Nina."

"*Please.*"

"Good girl." He wrapped his arms around her and worshipped her sweet little tits without restraint.

Nina was dying. Which was fine. Dying of pleasure turned out to be an excellent experience.

In the low light and the night-time quiet, her senses were flooded with James. The scent of him, that echo she'd smelled in his bed, was a thousand times as intense now that he held her tight. The heat of him, from his hard cock wedged between her thighs to his slick tongue circling her nipple, burned so beautifully. His growling moans as he pressed his face against her breasts made the tension in Nina's belly tighten, tighten, tighten. He was always so desperate for her, when they were like this. Surely that meant something. *Surely* it did.

Or maybe it didn't. But she wouldn't—couldn't—think about all that now. Not when he was wiping the bitterness of tonight's events away with his insistent hands. He cupped her arse, pressing her harder against his erection, grinding his hips with a wild need she understood perfectly. Nina clutched at his broad shoulders and matched him move for move, riding his dick through the layers of their underwear until she found the perfect angle.

When she moaned at the slow, rhythmic pressure, James looked up as if the ragged sound had called him. Their eyes met for a moment before he cradled her face in his hands and ... and ...

And nothing.

He'd been ready to kiss her. She'd swear it. For a second there, he'd thought about pressing his lips to hers. But in the end, he bent his head to kiss her throat instead. The coil of tension in Nina's stomach trembled and threatened to release, disappointment cooling blood that had been burning hot.

But then he spoke. He spoke, and she was back in the moment again, determined to take what he would give, even if it wasn't everything she wanted.

"Tell me what to do, Nina," he murmured. "You want to come? I'll make you come. You want me to lick that pretty pussy again?"

God, yes. *Yes*. But when she opened her mouth to say as much, something stopped her. A need even deeper than the desire for pleasure.

She wanted to pleasure *him*.

"Let me touch you," she whispered. *Let me give you something. Let me have what power I can over you, just for a little while.*

Maybe he heard all that she didn't say, because he hesitated. But only for a moment. Then he gave her what she craved.

"Yes," he said, and sat back.

Just one word, and the animal in her was released.

She swallowed as she leaned back to look at him. God, he was beautiful. In the silvery half-light the moon cast through their window, James glowed like some sort of fairy-tale prince. He was all pure, delicious darkness in the shadows, from his smooth skin to his hypnotic eyes. His full lips were slightly tilted in a teasing smile that made her heart skip a beat, but what really got her was his body.

His fucking *body*.

The barely restrained strength of it, and the softness too. He was comfort itself, power and gentleness, with his broad shoulders and heavy thighs, the curls of hair on his massive chest and the satisfying curve of his belly. She darted forward to kiss his nipples, first the left and then the right, tasting the raw sweetness of his skin with her tongue. When his breath hitched, she felt delicious satisfaction flare in her gut.

Yes, this was what she wanted: him. Piece by piece, moan by moan.

Her resolve strengthened, Nina began the kisses again—slowly, luxuriously, laving her tongue over the most sensitive parts of his body as she discovered them. The side of his throat, his biceps, his chest, belly, hips. She crawled off the sofa to kneel before him as she licked and sucked at the skin just above his briefs. When she turned her head, and her cheek brushed his dick through the fabric, James's whole body stiffened.

"Nina," he choked out, his hips rising and falling in an urgent rhythm. "Fuck, Nina, baby ..."

She almost moaned out loud at those words. Dragging his underwear off with one hand, she buried the other between her own thighs to stroke her desperate pussy. Couldn't stop, not when he was sitting there looking like that, kicking away his briefs and fisting his hard cock.

When he cupped the back of her head with one hand, Nina whimpered with pleasure, fingers circling her clit faster and faster. And when he pressed the gleaming head of his cock to her lips, she opened her mouth greedily.

"This what you want, sweetheart? You're sure?"

She'd barely finished the word "*Yes*" before he groaned and fed her that rigid length.

James tasted sharp and salty and perfect. His dick was as thick as the rest of him, already making her jaw ache, but the sensation didn't register as painful. No, to Nina, the insistent pressure of James filling her mouth to capacity was an erotic high. Her fingers slipped through her folds to her own tightening entrance, and she fucked herself in earnest, pressing the palm of her hand against her clit. Now her pussy stretched around her fingers, her mouth stretched around this man's magnificent dick, and God, she could come just like this.

But she wouldn't. Not yet. She wanted to stay lucid enough to taste it when he spurted down her throat.

So Nina sucked, hard and wet, as her mouth slid over James's cock. "Jesus," he hissed, dragging out the word. His eyes screwed shut in pleasure, his fist tightened in her hair, and the tendons in his neck strained as he threw back his head. Nina sucked again and again, graceless and desperate, and James grew wild beneath her, grunting and growling like an animal.

"Shit," he gasped, his eyes popping open. "You're gonna make me come. Slow down."

She slid off his length for a moment, breathless and loving it. "I want to make you come. Let me."

He studied her face for a moment before nodding. "If that's what you want, sweetheart."

Laughter bubbled up without permission. "Like it's not what *you* want."

His smile was sharp. "Anything I want becomes a thousand times better when you want it too, Nina. So if you want me to come down your throat—"

"Yes."

"Do me a favour. Keep playing with that wet little pussy for me. Make sure you come."

"Yes," she breathed again, and went back to sucking greedily on his cock.

In the end, they came together. James with a shout and a shudder, gasping her name as he pumped hot and wet into her mouth. And Nina, moaning around his erection, was pushed over the edge by the sight of him.

When they were done, he pulled her back into his lap and

held her tight and kissed her forehead, and for long, long moments, everything was absolutely perfect. She was dizzy with satisfaction, elated by it.

But then he kissed her head again, and sighed, and reached for her clothes. "You better go back to bed," he said. "Or you'll be knackered tomorrow. We both will."

And just like that, everything was shit again.

Chapter Eight

There weren't many people in her life that Nina considered accessible. Her brother was abroad being a tool of western imperialism, and her parents were retired dentists in Norfolk who scolded her for calling her brother a tool of western imperialism. (*Really*. It wasn't as if she blamed the individuals involved; it was the historic system she had a problem with.) She hated to bother her friends, almost as much as she hated to bother her family.

But she'd been forced to bother James, and it hadn't even ended badly. He was ... helping. Things were going well.

Well, except for the whole tragic, unrequited love thing. And the headfuck orgasms he threw out every so often.

Whatever.

The point was, she'd bothered James, and now here she was, days after the post-Bounce Nation fiasco, badgering someone else. Funny how it got easier—how it felt less like admitting defeat—every time.

James would probably call that growth.

"Rahul says we have to eat before we talk," Jasmine Allen informed Nina over her glossy coffee table. "He says that to do otherwise would make us as wild and lawless as animals, and he absolutely will not have it."

Across the open-plan living space, Jasmine's boyfriend, Rahul, gave her a pointed look over the breakfast bar. "That's not *exactly* how I phrased it, Jas." His expression was severe, all smooth brown skin over sharp, hawkish lines. But his eyes danced behind the frames of his glasses.

"That's what you meant, though," Jasmine insisted, throwing her bare legs over the arm of the corner sofa. "I could see it in your eyebrows!"

Nina choked down a laugh and snuck a sideways look at James. He was sitting next to her at the other end of the sofa, watching Jas and Rahul with a smile on his face. James was adorable when he smiled.

And wonderfully intimidating when he's protecting you.

But Nina wasn't supposed to think about the other night. Not the fear of that confrontation—or the dizzying, adrenaline-fuelled desire she'd grappled with afterwards.

She just couldn't figure James out. And maybe that problem could be resolved with something as basic as, you know, *talking* ... but for once in her life Nina couldn't make her runaway mouth work. She didn't dare to ask the difficult questions. She didn't dare to ask James *any* questions, because if his response was something along the lines of "I can't stop grabbing your arse because damn, girl, you eat your greens, but beyond that I feel nothing more than lust and friendship," she would have to do something dramatic, like ... cry.

So Nina had decided to ignore the entire issue. Even if that choice smacked of a cowardice she was unfamiliar with.

She curled her hands into loose fists and sat on them, just in case they took on a life of their own and decided to grab one of James's delicious pecs. He was looking dangerously yummy in today's mustard turtleneck and navy-blue braces. Plus, being around Jasmine and Rahul, with their mixture of easy affection and crackling intensity, was doing something terrible to Nina's resolve.

"Jas and Rahul were friends for seven years," she piped up suddenly, "before they got together. Did you know that?" *Do you care? Does it make you think of us?*

James stared at her for one heated, unreadable moment before turning a look of bland interest on the couple in question. "Bet that's quite a story," he said.

A story we could use as a blueprint, something reckless in Nina whispered. Maybe she should relocate her big-girl knickers and say it out loud sometime.

Did she dare?

Maybe the more important question was, could she bear not to?

"It *is* a story." Jasmine grinned. "A filthy one."

Jas was an oversharing kind of woman, though it never felt like oversharing because she was so charming. She had a golden ease about her that Nina had never mastered, one that came from being effortlessly adored. But that ease wasn't how their friendship had developed, quite the opposite. When they'd first met, through the non-profit where Jas gave legal aid to the vulnerable, Nina had been drawn to what lay beneath the other woman's sparkle.

Jasmine, despite all appearances to the contrary, hadn't lived a life without struggle.

But she was happy as a pig in shit these days, and had been ever since shacking up with her bossy best friend.

Speaking of the devil, Rahul wandered over with another of those disapproving, but strangely attractive, frowns. "Jas," he warned, before bending down to kiss her bare shoulder. "You're going to traumatise our guests. Sorry," he added to James. "She finds boundaries dull. It means she likes you."

James, to his credit, simply blinked, then burst out laughing.

Nina had a decent number of friends, but her tendency to keep them at arm's length meant they rarely met each other. She'd brought James along tonight because he refused to let her go anywhere alone—and because, truthfully, she hadn't wanted to be without him. But watching him fit in so easily with Jas and Rahul was causing all sorts of gooey, melty feelings in her belly, like her stomach had turned into chocolate fudge cake.

Dinner was served, and the conversation continued to meander in lazy, comfortable waves. Nina let it wash over her, her mind occupied by other things. She knew she should be thinking about her current situation—about the legal questions she had, and the connections Jas had made over the years that they might be able to utilise. About the plan Nina had spent the last two days hatching, partly so she wouldn't give in to her darkest urges and go back to that living room.

Instead, all she could think about was what she'd said to James: that Jasmine and Rahul had been friends for seven years before they'd gotten together.

And look at them. They were so obviously happy, so sickeningly meant for each other. It must have been nerve-wracking, risking a friendship as old and close as theirs. Must have been terrifying, wondering if a person you cared for so deeply on so many levels might not feel exactly the same. But they'd done it anyway. And their bravery had reaped rewards.

Nina's gaze drifted across the table without permission, landing on James as he sipped a glass of water and twirled pasta onto his fork. She watched his strong hands move, watched his throat bob as he swallowed. Then her questing gaze reached his eyes, so dark and familiar and dear. She loved those eyes. She loved *him*.

Enough to risk it all.

And that settled things, didn't it? As soon as this mess was over, as soon as she could breathe absolutely freely again ... Nina was going to claim what she wanted.

She was going to claim James.

"Nina?" She saw his mouth moving before she fully processed that he'd spoken. Jolting back down to earth, she realised the whole table was staring at her, their plates empty and their expressions concerned.

Except for Jasmine, who was flashing what appeared to be a knowing smirk. The cow.

"Nina?" James repeated, his voice louder, his brow furrowed.

"I'm fine," she said brightly. "Sorry. Fine. Just ..." She turned to Jasmine. "Shall we talk now?"

"About your situation? Yes. I have some thoughts on the doxing and tips on how we typically handle threats or presumed stalking," Jas said, rising from her seat. "Plus some ideas on executing the plan you texted me this morning. Shall we head to my office?"

Nina cleared her throat and nodded, bustling after a suddenly businesslike Jas. But when she reached the doorway, she turned back to glance at James.

And found him watching her with the kind of intensity he usually saved for their secret moments in the dark.

When she caught him, he faltered for the barest second, but he didn't look away. Instead, he lifted his chin and held her gaze steadily, almost as if he wanted to see her reaction.

Maybe she wasn't the only one feeling a little inspired by Jas and Rahul.

James spent the next two days thinking hard about the bright, fragile note in Nina's voice when she'd said, *"Jas and Rahul were friends for seven years."* And the next two nights staring at the living room door, praying she'd come, praying she wouldn't.

What did it mean that she stayed away?

He was starting to get sick of never-ending questions and assumptions. So sick he might just fucking ask her.

They were adults. Nina was the most sensible woman he knew, heroine complex aside. If he didn't want to spend the rest of his life blue in the balls, or ashamed of the things he did with her in silence and in darkness, or fucking pining until he wasted away into a mix of air and hope, *he should just fucking ask her.* Fear be damned. James was in the middle of repeating that mantra to himself when she got the phone call.

He was with Nina when the phone rang—or rather, she was with him, sitting in the old Volvo he was working on, tapping away at her laptop. He was supposed to be concentrating, but he'd spent most of his morning watching her. Thinking about her. Wondering if it was possible to believe so wholly in your own negative assumptions that you could miss something perfect sitting right in front of you.

When the phone's tinny ringtone sounded, Nina jumped as if she'd just been hit by lightning. He watched her squint at the screen—and then, unexpectedly, her antisocial glare melted into excitement.

Their eyes met through the windscreen, and he arched an eyebrow. Mouthed, *"Police?"*

She shook her head, set her laptop aside, and took the call. He could hear her half of the conversation loud and clear, but that wasn't enough to tell him what was going on. "Yes, this is she. That's correct. Oh, of course. Yes. Thank you." There was a slight pause, and then she began again. "Hello! Antonina Chapman. Charmed."

Charmed? Her phone voice was in full effect.

"Thank you so much for picking up my little story. No,

absolutely. Oh, well, you've got to keep your chin up, haven't you, in situations like these? Although ..." She hesitated, then spoke again, her voice wavering. "Obviously, it's been difficult at times. I—um—sorry, sorry." She pressed her lips together and cleared her throat.

James dropped his torque wrench, the vulnerability in her voice calling him like a dog whistle. *Nina's upset. Fix it.* But then she looked up, caught his eye, raised a hand palm-first in the universal sign for "*stop*".

And winked.

He hesitated, baffled.

She kept speaking in that wispy, stuttering voice. "Thank you. Yes, of course. It all started with my analysis of the recent Brexit scandal, when the Leave campaign was proven to have made false claims and promises. I truly believe in disseminating information, making it accessible to all—that's why I so admire you and what you do. I feel that we have the same aims, sharing genuine facts with normal people. Yes. Yes, exactly. So, I shared the article, but ..." She sobbed gently. The sound stabbed at James's heart, even though he was beginning to suspect that this whole thing was an act. "I suppose it gained the wrong sort of attention. You know what Brexit does to people. And now ..."

Nina launched into a stilted explanation of the last few weeks, her words dripping with more emotion than she typically displayed in a month. And she was, apparently, talking to a *stranger*. Knowing her the way he did, James was certain that she must be painfully uncomfortable. Mortified. Which also meant that whatever she was up to, she had a damned good reason for it.

When she finally put the phone down, after a series of inane and repetitive farewells, he stalked over to her side of the car and opened the door. "What the hell was that?"

"That was Jasmine getting me a slot on *Good Morning*

Ladies with Heidi Carpenter."

At the name of the famous breakfast chat show host, his jaw dropped. "*What?*"

"What?"

He scowled at her faux-innocent expression. "Heidi Carpenter? *The* Heidi Carpenter?"

"Yep." Nina lifted her hips and slid her phone into her back pocket. For once, even the way her thighs flexed wasn't enough to distract him. Much.

"You're going to be a guest on *Good Morning Ladies*?"

"Yes." She gave him a winning smile. It was the fakest expression he'd ever seen on her face, but if you didn't know her, it would look pretty.

Very pretty.

"I'm going to disclose my harrowing ordeal and win Middle Britain's hearts and minds," she said cheerfully.

After a pause in which he grappled with his pure astonishment, James choked out, "When?"

"Three days."

"*How?*"

She smirked as if she'd been waiting for him to ask. "Persuasion. It's all righteous, faux-woke bullshit, but that's okay. They exploit me and my story, I get public support and short-term hyper-visibility, AKA relative safety, in return. Who needs police when you've got paps?"

"So the ... the crying was part of the *persuasion?*"

"The *almost*-crying," she corrected. "But not quite, because I'm so very brave and composed." At his baffled expression, she sighed and broke things down. "I know what these people value in a woman. Fragility is currency, but I'm not pale enough to be permitted *too* much delicacy."

He grimaced. "How the hell do you know this stuff?"

"Life. Also, you think I twiddled my thumbs throughout my

journalism degree or something?" God, she looked so smug. He loved it.

"Lots of people have journalism degrees, Cupcake. I don't see them popping up on morning television whenever they like."

She rolled her eyes. "Maybe because those people don't also have years of social media expertise, a solid platform, and a story that'll make the average Joe feel better about himself for doing the bare minimum in the fight for equality. And Jasmine, of course. Most people don't have Jasmine. She knows a horrific amount of people and they all love her terribly."

James nodded, feeling slightly dazed. Why did he enjoy it so much when Nina went into professional, capable mode? Well, he knew *why*—because capable women turned him on, and Nina was the queen of capable. But understanding his weaknesses didn't make them any less inappropriate. He was supposed to be supporting her here, like a *friend*, not drooling over her.

Maybe she wouldn't mind both.

Maybe not. But this probably wasn't the time to find out. Even if something in his chest tugged at its chains and demanded to know when *would* be the time.

Later.

"You think it'll help?" James asked.

"I know it will. Visibility can be dangerous, but the *right* kind of visibility is like a shield."

"Alright then," he murmured, nodding slowly as he absorbed everything. "In that case ... I guess we should celebrate tonight."

Her tongue snaked out to wet her lower lip, a smooth glide over lush skin. For a moment, he wondered if she was reading something into his suggestion—something more interesting than a takeaway.

She smiled and said, "Dinner's on you."

Chapter Nine

F unny how quickly things could turn on their head. For the first time in a long time, Nina felt exactly like herself— powerful, invincible, ready for anything. Or maybe a new and improved version of herself, since she now realised it was okay to reclaim those feelings with a little help.

James was adding to her current high by acting as if she was the smartest, most successful person in the world. He beamed at her all day until they locked up the garage and went home. He ordered Thai food because gang jay was her favourite, even though she knew he'd prefer curry goat. He even got two lots of chips so she didn't have to share—and then, to top it all off, he pulled up *Buffy* on Netflix.

"Seriously?" she asked, her grin unstoppable. "Even though you think Angel's a creep?"

"Even though I think Angel's a creep," he agreed. "And even though someone needs to call Social Services on Buffy's mother. This is your night, Cupcake."

And she was so thoroughly content, she couldn't even scowl at him for calling her that.

Although, as the evening rolled on and night fell outside

their window, Nina did notice a *little* chip in her newfound contentment—the same one that had been there before.

Everything was perfect, except for the fact that James wasn't hers.

Yet, whispered that little streak of invincibility inside her.

The growing darkness was thrusting her back in time, back into her memories of seeing James, touching James, right here on this sofa. She shifted on the cushions, giddy nerves and remembered arousal making her restless. Crossed her legs, uncrossed them, flicked a look at him, then stared rigidly back at the screen. She knew what she was going to do. Couldn't stop herself, not even a little bit. Now was the time. Double or nothing.

The only problem was, she couldn't quite figure out a smooth way to do it. Romantic relationships were not Nina's area of expertise. How exactly did one start the *"Hey, I've been thinking, and you might be it for me"* conversation? She couldn't think, not while her nerves continued to insist in Eeyore-like tones that she was about to be rejected once and for all.

Because at the end of the day, this was real life. And in real life, happy endings weren't guaranteed. Friendship plus sexual chemistry plus the indescribable energy that whirled between them did not necessarily equal romance. People, she reminded herself, could be platonic soulmates.

But platonic soulmates didn't accidentally make each other come. Did they? Maybe they did. She didn't know much about the whole thing. She'd Google it.

Or you could ask him, Chapman.

Well, yes. There was that.

Nina cleared her throat. But when she spoke, her voice still sounded hoarse, cracked, on edge. "James?"

He gave her a questioning look that ... changed, after a moment. As if he'd seen something in her face. That something made him wordlessly pause the TV, made him turn toward her on the sofa, their knees brushing. Which was inconvenient, since even the slightest physical contact with him made her stomach flutter and her train of thought list slightly to the left.

"Nina?" he asked softly, his gaze burning. His hand found hers on the sofa cushion, and slowly, cautiously, he tangled their fingers together. The action, and the feel of his warm, calloused palm, loosened the last of the nerves in her chest. James made it easy to be brave. He made her drunk on the urge to match him, to give him what he deserved. Because this man's natural restraint didn't stop him from reaching out to her again and again when she truly needed it.

And now she knew she was strong enough to offer him that same vulnerability.

"Do you know," she asked slowly, "what you mean to me?"

Something flared in his gaze. He shifted forward almost infinitesimally, then back again, as if barely containing himself. His throat moved as he swallowed, hard.

"I think," he rasped after a moment, "that you could tell me."

"I adore you," she croaked, the words foreign and stiff, squeezed awkwardly from her throat as if she'd forced squares through circular holes.

He smiled, slow and—though he probably didn't realise it—sexy as hell. "*Do* you now?"

"Oh, fuck off." She rolled her eyes and turned away.

"No, no, keep going."

"I have nothing else to say," she insisted primly—but that wasn't true. She had so much to say that she was overflowing with it, but the heat and the happiness in his eyes were making her think that James might actually want what she was about to offer. And that possibility, which had seemed so impossible for all this time, was somehow making her even more nervous than she had been before.

No, Nina didn't understand it either. Apparently, caring about people—in the personal way, not the principles-of-basic-human-goodness way—turned her into a scared little baby. Ick.

"Liar," James murmured, as if he'd read her mind. As if he saw the secrets she was tempted to swallow. The tenderness in his voice said he didn't mind her hesitation, that he'd guide her through it.

Then he caught her by the waist and pulled her into his arms. She squeaked in surprise and grabbed his shoulders automatically—but it only took a second for Nina to settle in like she belonged there, her thighs straddling his effortlessly. Just the act of spreading her legs around him made something tighten low in her belly. She pressed her fingers into hard muscle and bit her lip. Met his gaze and fought not to shiver at how close they were, his breaths ghosting over her skin, the slight edge of hunger in his expression impossible to miss.

That hunger grew easier and easier to see every time they touched. And Nina was starting to think about those times as something other than a mistake, something other than James's biggest regret or the sin he couldn't resist. She'd been so caught up in her own worries that she'd forgotten how steady, how solid, how consistent James Foster really was. But now she remembered: no matter what else changed, this man was always utterly, resolutely himself. And the simple fact was that James didn't do casual sex.

Yet he'd fallen to his knees before her and dragged off her clothes and buried his face in her cunt. He'd stroked himself to orgasm while holding her gaze. He'd thrust into her mouth like he couldn't do anything but.

So what, exactly, did that mean?

Her mind racing, she wrapped her arms around him and

buried her face against his throat. "You know," she murmured into the vibrating silence, "you're incredibly huggable."

His hands settled at her hips and squeezed. She felt his dick swelling beneath her, waited for him to push her away and try to hide it.

He didn't.

Instead James stayed right where he was, massive dick and all, his grip on her tight and possessive. He asked with a dark note of amusement in his voice, "Huggable? Is that what they call guys like me these days?"

"Maybe." She tried to ignore the sensation spiralling from his touch—this was supposed to be a soft and mushy conversation, not a Horny Nina conversation. It wasn't as if he'd just grabbed her tits, for Christ's sake. And yet his big hands resting on her hips felt unbearably erotic.

If they were naked like this, he'd be gripping her tight and pushing her down onto his shaft.

She swallowed, pushing the thought away for later. "'Bear' would probably fit, too."

He pulled back and arched an eyebrow. "Which means ...?"

"You really don't know?"

"I'm a lot older than you," he sighed. "I don't know all this slang shit."

"First of all, six and a half years is not a lot. Jesus, you're so dramatic."

"And second of all?" His smile was a blatant tease.

There was no bloody second of all. With as much dignity as she could manage, Nina sniffed, "Some things are said purely for dramatic effect, you know."

He laughed, and in that moment, he was so achingly beautiful that the force of her need almost broke her. She put a hand to his face, unable to stop herself, hypnotised by the sight of his joy—the curve of his full lips, the freedom in his smile, the lines cradling his dark eyes. He calmed slowly, his laughter fading until nothing but white-hot intensity remained.

"Nina," he said softly, and that one word let her know that everything was about to change. "I adore you too. I think my biggest fear might be losing you."

Her heart constricted. Something fluttered in her chest, a mixture of longing and panic. She bit her lip bloodless and kept her hand against his cheek and ... hoped.

Sometimes, hope worked.

"I was so afraid," he went on steadily, his voice low and rough with emotion, "that I let fear make me a coward. But you know what, Cupcake? I don't think it suits me."

She swallowed. Hard. "Funny. I've been thinking the same thing about myself."

One of James's hands slid under her T-shirt to touch her bare skin. He swept his thumb over the curve of her hip, and a mortifying little whimper tumbled from her lips. What was it about this man? Was it the way he looked her in the eye as he touched her, like he was starving for every little reaction? Was it the slow, tantalising ease with which he teased out her responses?

Or was it the love she'd kept locked up in her chest until it grew too huge to hide or contain or deny?

Um, yeah, probably that last one.

"James," she blurted out, with no idea what she might say next, except that it would probably be embarrassingly honest.

Except he got there first.

"I want you," he said. "I'm not talking about sex, Nina. I want *you*. Bad. I can think of a thousand reasons why I shouldn't, but I've been trying to stop for a while, and I can't, so I guess none of those reasons really matter. I just need to know if you want me too—"

"I do," she said, breathless, giddy, her mind scrambled with pleasure. Her fingers curled into the fabric of his shirt as if part of her feared this moment might be yanked away as suddenly as it had come.

"But *how*?" His fingers slid over her throat in a possessive hold she'd never felt from him before—but he'd come close, she remembered; often, he'd come close. He was always holding onto her in a thousand little ways, touching her more firmly than a friend might.

And she'd missed every signal. Or maybe he'd just hidden them well beneath that calm, reasonable façade.

"How do you want me?" he demanded. "Because half-measures aren't an option. I told you once I can't be like those boys you take to bed. I can't be that to you. I won't. And if that's all you're offering, I'm not—I won't take it." He forced the words out between clenched teeth as if they hurt to say, but still, he said them. "We'll just have to go back to the way it was before. I'll still be here, Nina. But when it comes to this ... this *thing* between us, I'm all or nothing."

And with that, for the very first time, she understood. Everything. The hesitation, the dance of hot-and-cold they'd been doing, why she'd been unable to figure James out for the first time in her life. It had never occurred to her that he might honestly believe she'd put him in the same category as any other man in her life. He wasn't like anyone else. Not in any way. But obviously, she hadn't been very good at showing him that.

Hadn't been brave enough to show him that.

She would be, though. For him, from this moment on, she fucking would be.

She traced a shaking thumb over his lower lip and let her question escape on a whisper. "Why don't you trust me, James?"

"I trust you completely." She felt his answer as much as she heard it, his breath shivering over her hand.

"But you think I'd hurt you?" she asked softly. "You don't think I know what you need?"

Shock flitted through his gaze. He took a deep breath, his chest rising visibly. "We—before the first time you kissed me, Nina, you and I have never been like this." But his voice caught. And the words were jagged, harsh. And his eyes burned.

"Are you lying to me, James?"

His jaw hardened.

"Are you trying to say, before the first time we touched, you'd never thought about fucking me? That when I caught you looking at me like you wanted to bite, that was all in my head?" Her words came out hot and slow, and each one seemed to pain him.

"I ... shouldn't have. I shouldn't now."

"Because?"

"I've known you too long. We're friends. You're Markus's—" He sucked in a breath. "But shit, Nina, the problem is—the problem has been for a while now—that I don't fucking care. This is complicated, and if it goes sideways it'll be messy as shit and it will fucking destroy me, and I. Don't. Care."

Nina hadn't thought she could smile this wide. But apparently, her face was capable of incredible things when she had a gorgeous man at her mercy, listing all the reckless ways he wanted her. Leaning forward until her lips brushed his, she whispered, "Good."

He released a shaking breath, one that shimmered with all the need and tenderness burning between them. "Nina," he said, his voice low and rough. "What are you trying to do here?"

"I'd think it was obvious," she murmured. "I don't chase men, but I've been chasing the hell out of you. You don't do casual—" She broke off with a moan as his hand tightened around her throat, his thumb stroking over her pulse. "God, James, that's hot."

"Glad to hear it. Now finish your sentence before I die."

She huffed out a laugh. "You don't do casual, and I don't want casual with you. James ... I'd never risk our friendship for something I could get anywhere else. This is it. This is more."

He closed his eyes, a frown creasing his brow. "Nina. Baby. Please tell me you mean it. Because if I get my hands on you again, sweetheart ... letting go won't be easy, let's put it that way."

He couldn't possibly know how those words lit her up inside, how they sent an answering dart of possessiveness through her. "Good."

He opened his eyes. Their gazes clashed, his warm brown to her near-black. And then the lust between them, an electrical current dancing just beneath the surface of every interaction, surged to life.

James kissed her. He kissed her, and it was everything.

Chapter Ten

How had he ever denied himself this?

Nina was explosive in his arms, her lips soft and sweet against his, her taste utterly intoxicating. James couldn't think beyond the sensation of her tongue teasing his mouth, her hands grabbing his shirt, her soft body pressed against his. But somehow, he maintained enough awareness to decide that he was not about to love her on this fucking sofa again. This time, he'd have her in a bed. And this time, he wouldn't stop.

She wanted him. She wanted *him*, truly and completely, and he knew her well enough to realise that she wouldn't break his heart—not on purpose, anyway. If she was asking for this, she meant it. And if she meant it, he could take the risk.

Fuck, he wanted this woman so bad, he'd have tried to seduce her into love even if all she wanted was a quick fuck. But apparently, she wanted ... more.

"This is it," she'd said.

And it would be. James planned to make sure of that.

He swept Nina up into his arms, laughing when she gasped against his mouth, and carried her to the bedroom so fast, he barely remembered the journey. All at once she was lying in his bed, where she belonged, and he was sliding between her thighs where *he* belonged, and their lips met again, and heaven came down to earth just for them.

"Take this off," she panted, pulling at his shirt.

"Take *these* off," he countered, dragging down her sweats.

"Stop, stop, stop." She laughed and pushed him up into a sitting position. "Get up. Get naked. Find a condom."

He stood and dragged his shirt over his head. "While we're giving out orders, you should get naked too."

"On it." She was already kicking off her bottoms. He paused for a moment, mesmerised by the movement of her soft, lush thighs, and then she parted her legs and he saw the wetness darkening her underwear.

He gave a hoarse groan, his head falling back. "Woman. Jesus."

"Concentrate on your assigned tasks, please," she said, pulling her top over her head. He was so hard, so thoroughly distracted by the bounce of her suddenly naked tits, that he almost missed the hint of laughter in her voice. "If we both stay foc—*James!*"

He couldn't help it. He was still wearing his boxers when he pounced on her, and he didn't have a condom yet, but he couldn't be expected to follow instructions when she was sitting there looking like that. Nina lay beneath him, laughing helplessly as he straddled her. His focus was split between her smile—she was so fucking beautiful when she smiled—and her breasts, sweet handfuls with tight nipples that belonged between his lips. When he bent his head and flicked his tongue over one blackberry tip, her laughter turned into a low, husky moan and her hands slid down to cup his head.

"Oh," she sighed, "yeah. You can stay there."

"Just here?" He looked up, arched an eyebrow, and reached

between their bodies to palm the wet heat of her pussy. "Are you sure?"

Nina bit her lip. "No? Maybe? No. See, this is why we were supposed to focus."

"I'm completely focused," he said, which was true. He was focused on getting her naked, making her come, and pushing his hard, aching cock inside her. In that order. Maybe with a few extra orgasms thrown in. To that end, he bent his head and sucked her nipple fully into his mouth, even as his hands worked to pull off her underwear. She arched her back, pushing her tits in his face, and he decided that the scent of her skin might be more vital to him than oxygen. Then, her underwear finally disposed of, she wrapped her thighs around him. He felt the hot, slippery kiss of her cunt through his boxers, scalding his dick and tightening his balls and sending sparks of desperate pleasure down his spine. If her skin was oxygen, her pussy must be life itself.

He couldn't lose his head, though. This was for her. Everything he did was for her. So James resisted the urge to kiss his way down her body and bury his face between her legs, even though he was pretty sure she'd enjoy it—and even though he still remembered, still *dreamed* about the intoxicating taste of her. Raising his head to look at her, gritting his teeth against the hunger that pounded through his bloodstream, he asked, "What do you want, sweetheart?"

She blinked up at him with lust-drugged eyes, relaxed in a way he'd never seen before. She trusted him. The thought made his heart swell, made him prouder than anything he'd ever done. Then her legs tightened around him and she rocked against his painful erection and he had very few thoughts beyond *fuck* and *Nina* and *now*.

"I want *you*," she said, her voice hoarse and urgent. "Just— James, can you just fuck me? I know you probably want to do all that romantic shit, and I'm cool with that, but right now I really, *really* need your dick in me, so ... um ... what are you doing?"

He was reaching over her, opening his bedside drawer and grabbing a box of condoms, that's what the fuck he was doing.

"I'm with you on that," he said, ripping a latex packet open with his teeth. "We're fucking. Your wish is my command. Etcetera." He rose up on his knees, shoved down his boxers and went to roll on the condom, but she stopped him, covering his hand with hers. He looked up to find Nina staring at his dick like it was dessert, her dark gaze lingering on the swollen head, the gleam of pre-come, the fine veins standing out against his skin. He was really fucking hard. Really. Fucking. Hard. And so turned on that when she licked her bottom lip, his dick actually twitched. He clenched his jaw at the stab of sheer lust that went through him, tried not to come all over her pretty face right then and there ...

But Nina slid a hand between her thighs and circled her own clit with a finger, and his control shattered.

"Fuck," he gritted out, rolling on the condom with a speed he hadn't known he was capable of. "I need inside that pussy before I lose it."

She spread her legs wider, kept stroking herself. "Hurry up, then." Her voice was a ragged whisper. Her folds glistened, all slick and soft and open for him, like the best kind of taunt. God, he felt dizzy.

Moving fast, James covered her body with his, holding his weight on one hand, using the other to grab her thigh and spread her even wider. "Ready, baby?"

"Yes," she breathed, her hips lifting, searching him out.

"Keep touching yourself," he ordered. "Tell me if it hurts—"

"Maybe I want it to hurt."

"Shit, Nina. Unless you want me to come before you get any dick whatsoever, keep that to yourself."

She laughed, but the sound cut short when his cock found her entrance. He bent his head to kiss her pretty, filthy mouth, and as her tongue met his, James pushed.

It was a slow, easy glide into Nina's tight cunt, her wet heat welcoming him like they'd been made to fit together. "Ohhh, fuck," he hissed. He hadn't meant to; pure bliss dragged those words out of him. It felt as if his lungs had seized, his heart had stopped, the world had paused, and he was frozen in a shard of impossible, sharp-edged perfection. Then, all at once, the moment passed. But he couldn't forget that feeling—not when Nina was soft beneath him, her pussy hot around him, her hands demanding as she pulled him closer. Then she kissed him again, and he'd never known anything so divine as this, as having her everywhere in every way.

Driven by mindless, frantic need, he thrust. Hard.

Nina had kind of expected James to fuck her brains out, but she hadn't been ready for this. No one could be ready for this.

Her need for him was ravenous and wild and it had teeth. When his thick cock shoved deep inside her, the sweet friction and the eventual, *perfect* glide made her toes curl. Tendrils of pleasure tightened around her limbs and held her hostage, every muscle in her body straining under the ruthless pleasure he gave her. But even that wasn't enough to assuage the need. Not yet.

So she clung to him and met him thrust for thrust, revelling in his warmth and his strength and the raw, guttural sounds he made as he pounded into her. When he lowered his head to suck her nipples again, she could've cried. His tongue swirling around her sensitive areola and his dick sliding over her G-spot and his pelvis rocking against her clit all conspired against her until she was practically sobbing, gasping out things she'd never thought she could say. *"Oh my God, oh my God, I need you forever, don't stop, don't ever stop, I can't take it, fuck, James."* On and on, her pleasure spilled out like an ocean overflowing, and then, somehow, he made it worse.

Raising his lips to her ear, he talked back. And he talked dirty.

"Tell me, sweetheart. Tell me how good I fuck you."

She'd love to, except she was suddenly unable to speak. All she could do was pant and moan pathetically, and rock against him desperately as pleasure rose to a crescendo.

And still, he talked, his voice smoke and whisky and hot, dark nights. "Jesus, Nina, you feel so good. And so fucking wet. I wish I could taste you and fuck you at the same time." He rode her thoroughly. Pressed a hot kiss to her throat, then another, then another, until sensation zipped over her tender skin and her moans became ragged and desperate. "We might have to get creative," he murmured. "I want to hold you down and suck your clit until you cry. Watch you fuck yourself on a dildo for me. I want a lot of things from you, love."

Hopefully one of them was an orgasm, because at that moment, she came.

James held her by the throat and fucked her through it. While her body shook and her pussy spasmed and her breath was forced from her lungs through sheer pleasure, he thrust into her again and again, so deep she felt it in her chest, so perfect she could die right then and have no regrets. And when he choked out her name a moment later, and held her to him, and found his release, she felt happier and deliciously filthier than she ever had in her life.

After that, time passed in a gentle haze of blurred vision and loose limbs. She felt the mattress shift as he got up, smiled dreamily when he kissed her forehead and murmured that he wouldn't be a second. And then she might have fallen asleep a little bit.

At some point she came back down to earth and found herself lying on her back, her sweat-damp skin cooling ... until James slung one heavy thigh over her hips and wrapped his arms around her. Just like that, she was dragged under by his intoxicating scent and surrounded by his warmth, safer than she'd ever felt before. But even though she loved the position, she couldn't pass up the opportunity to take the piss.

"So you're a snuggler," she said. "Interesting."

"If you intend to complain," he replied, his voice muffled against her hair, "just know that I'm not above kissing you to keep you quiet."

She laughed, until an anxiety-inducing thought popped into her head, drowning out the amusement. "So, that was ... And now, we ... Which means ..." She cleared her throat and thought wistfully of a time, less than twenty-four hours ago, when she'd been quite articulate. Jesus, how did people do this romantic shit when they cared so much about it?

Then again, Nina supposed, she was no stranger to caring about things. And *this* thing mattered more, mattered most—so she had to pull herself together and be brave. "James," she said firmly. "I know we talked about feelings and stuff, but, erm, what is this?"

He laughed gently, and held her tighter, which she hadn't thought was possible. "You and me, you mean?"

"Yeah."

"I'd like to think we're in a relationship. What do you think about that?"

Peace fell like spring rain, dragging a goofy smile over Nina's face. "I think I agree," she said, trying not to sound too delighted. "A relationship. Yeah." And then she added wryly, "Can't wait to tell my brother."

"Bedroom rule," James said. "We don't talk about your brother."

She snorted. "Fair enough. But we do have to tell—"

James's hand covered her mouth, not hard enough to really shut her up, but she got the message. Got it, and ignored it. With wicked amusement, she said against his palm, "You were supposed to be watching me."

"I did watch you," he said. "I watched you bend over in those jeans with the rip underneath your right arse cheek."

"James!"

"You know what? I don't really care what Mark thinks, because you're an adult. And I know you don't care either, so stop breaking the bedroom rule." He moved his hand away from her mouth, setting the sound of her laughter free. Then, without warning, he shifted until he was on top of her, his sinful smile bright and beautiful. "Your official punishment," he said seriously, "is one kiss."

"Just one?"

"I'll thank you not to diminish my excellent kisses. One is definitely enough."

She laughed and took her punishment. James's mouth was surprisingly sweet and achingly gentle against hers, transforming the glitter of her amusement into something slower, hotter, more needy. As his tongue traced her lower lip, Nina's arousal flared—but that was nothing compared to the other currents flooding her mind, the fond affection and the deep possessiveness and ...

Suddenly, she was so full of feeling she couldn't possibly keep it in. Breaking the kiss, she blurted out, "I love you."

Of course, once she'd said it, she really wished that she hadn't.

For a moment of perfect, shining mortification, Nina might've sacrificed a sheep—a small goat, at least—for the chance to cram those words back into her mouth. And since she'd been a vegetarian since she was fourteen, that was a pretty major concession.

But once that moment passed, she realised that actually, she'd rather not sacrifice any goats. It was better this way. *She* was better brave. And she'd already started, so she might as well go all in. Gnawing on her lower lip, avoiding James's gaze—his chest was a lot easier to stare at right now than his eyes—she kept talking.

"I've been in love with you for, like, three years. I don't know. It kind of snuck up on me. But I thought you'd never see me in that way, so I tried to ignore it, and then I got this ridiculous idea about, like, seducing you." She laughed nervously, her voice higher than usual. She had to keep talking, had to stretch out the moment in time when she was still doing this to avoid the moment in time when it would be utterly, awkwardly *done.* "Obviously, that didn't go very well—you kind of took it the wrong way—and I got pretty sensitive about the whole thing, I'm not gonna lie—I mean, you weren't *obligated* to want me—"

"Nina," James interrupted gently.

She ignored him, shifting onto her back and staring at the smooth white ceiling. "But all that doesn't really matter now, because you do want me, except of course you might have changed your mind a little bit now because—"

"No, Nina."

"Because really, who just says they—"

"I love you," James said.

She froze. Shock sent her mind haywire until all she could splutter in response was, "Are you serious?"

"About loving you?" he asked mildly.

"No, about your choice in wallpaper. *Yes,* about loving me."

"Antonina Chapman." He smiled. "I am absolutely serious about loving you."

James was almost always serious, after all. And yet, she turned to stare into his eyes, as if she might spot doubt or hesitation. Instead, all she saw was steady, shining affection—deep enough, vast enough, heavy enough to scare her and wrap her up safe and sound all at the same time. She pressed a hand to his cheek, feeling the rasp of stubble beneath her palm. "Really?"

His hand settled on *her* cheek and they were mirrors of each other. "Really."

Smiling now, she narrowed her eyes. "You're not just saying that to make me feel better?" She knew he wasn't. She knew.

James burst out laughing, his whole body shaking with it, his smile brighter than the sun. "Oh, for God's sake, Nina. Come here."

And she did, because she knew he meant it. James Foster did not lie to Nina Chapman. That much was almost law between them.

And here, now, as their lips met, was a new law. Freshly forged, but no less powerful than all the rest.

They loved each other. They loved each other. They loved each other.

Epilogue

"It's been difficult, to say the least."

James stood backstage and watched Nina's face on the small flat screen. After an hour in hair and makeup, she looked beautiful, if kind of ... un-Nina-like. But she knew what she was doing. If she'd allowed someone to put her thick hair into a neat braid, even though the style gave her headaches, there must be a reason. And if she'd let them slather lip gloss all over her, and was even remembering not to lick it off, there must be a reason. So he didn't focus on the differences, or even on the delicate, fluttering movements she made with her hands, or the calculated pauses in her speech. He focused on her words.

Because, with her clever performance, Nina was saying the kind of things no one got away with saying on TV.

"Of course." Heidi Carpenter nodded, her mouth a moue of sympathetic understanding. "I mean, the kind of abuse you've received ..." She paused to glance at the vast screen behind the deceptively homey-looking sofa she and Nina were perched on. A scrolling view of the messages, tweets and comments Nina had gotten appeared, the profanity blurred until the whole thing was a sea of smudged black and white. "It must have shaken you."

"It did," Nina said softly. "It did." And though this whole thing was a performance of a kind, a calculation, another kind of strength—he heard the truth there, too. Nina's vulnerability wasn't for anyone else, but it still existed. Whether she hid it or used it or chose to ignore it, it was always there.

"The thing is," she went on, "I consider myself to be a tough woman. I have a support network, too, people around me who love and protect me. But if I were more fragile, or alone, this could truly have torn me apart. Sometimes I think Black women in particular are seen as 'strong' in a way that removes our humanity. There have been some extreme examples in the media lately—think Prince Ruben and his wife, Cherry Neita, or the furore around the Duke and Duchess of Sussex. People believe that abusing us doesn't matter, because we can take more than other people. That's not the case. My real worry is for the Black girls and young women who'll see the messages I've received and wonder if those insults apply to them. That's how hate poisons entire societies."

Heidi hummed supportively before saying, "And what about those who are purely concerned with your politics? Because, as we've seen, some of the messages you received were atrocious—but there are others who have no problem with you personally, yet suggest that your beliefs are dangerous."

Nina gave a small laugh, her dark eyes sparkling with what James knew was true amusement. She was handling all this very well, but she'd stayed up most of last night with nerves. She hadn't been able to eat breakfast that morning. But now, she was laughing, and it was real, and he'd never been so proud of her.

She could find humour anywhere, despite her constant analysis of the world's darkness. He didn't think she realised how precious that was, but he'd make sure to remind her.

"I'm far from dangerous," she said, her lips still curved into a sweet little smile. "I want education for all and honest government. My only rule is 'do no harm'. If anyone doubts that, all they have to do is read my website and formulate an opinion for themselves."

"Well," Heidi said with a coy little glance at the camera, "you certainly don't seem scary to me!"

Nina laughed again, and if he hadn't known her so well, he'd have had no idea that this one was fake. "What rankles," she said, "is that I'm being treated as a threat for writing an article about the Leave campaign's proven duplicity—which is something I think Britain deserves to know about. Our government representatives should work for us, not trick us."

Heidi nodded in silent—and therefore not-too-controversial—agreement.

"I don't think sharing public information is dangerous," Nina went on. "What's truly dangerous is the fact that someone attempted to dox me. That I've had online threats and harassment leak into my real life. Where's the outcry against the people who threatened to kill me? The ones who've spent weeks terrorising me?" Her words were quiet, but that somehow made her passion more compelling.

"That's an excellent question," Heidi said. "I, for one, am disgusted. But, Nina, we're running out of time here, so I'd like to end on a question for *you*: you're very young, and yet you've been writing about politics and social issues for years now. It doesn't seem like any of your goals for the nation have come to fruition—in fact, with developments like Brexit and the current Tory government, things have been moving in the opposite direction. How does that make you feel?"

Nina looked straight at the camera, a sad smile on her face. "It makes me feel like the unfairness in the world may never end. But that's okay, because hope never dies."

Hope never dies.

She was wonderful. She was incredible. She was *vital.*

James had no doubt that Nina's life would be extraordinary and her legacy brilliant. The world needed people like Antonina Chapman.

But all James needed was Nina.

Want More Sexy, Diverse Romance?

Turn the page for a sneak peek at my steamy, emotional romance *A Girl Like Her*, in which a prickly heroine who's despised by her small town tries to resist the sweet hero who just moved in next door...

A Girl Like Her

"You shouldn't do that, you know."

Evan Miller stifled a sigh.

He didn't need to look over his shoulder to know who those words had come from. After five days at Burne & Co., he was more familiar with those cultured, charming tones than he'd like.

So Evan continued to focus on the length of iron before him, holding it up to the light, making sure that he'd drawn it out just far enough. His muscles ached and sweat trailed down his brow as the forge cooled. He was almost ready to leave, but now he wanted to find some reason to stay. Just ten more minutes, or maybe twenty. As long as it took for his visitor to get the hint.

Evan had been waiting all week for Daniel Burne to lose interest in him, and so far it didn't seem to be working. Maybe Evan was the problem. Maybe, by not rushing to befriend the boss's kid, he'd made himself stand out too much.

Daniel Burne was rich, handsome, good at his job despite the possible nepotism, and king of this small town. He probably didn't understand why Evan rebuffed his friendship. That was the problem with popular people; they needed, more than anything, to be noticed.

So it came as no surprise when, instead of going away, Daniel moved further into the workshop. He wandered within Evan's line of sight and leant against the wall, folding his arms.

This time, Evan didn't stifle his sigh. He released it loudly, a drawn-out gust that spoke a thousand words. But his mother had raised him to be a gentleman, so that sigh was the only hint of annoyance that he allowed to escape.

"What's up?" Evan asked, lowering the iron finial.

Daniel's auburn hair gleamed bright in the light of the dying fire. He tossed his head toward the line of cooling finials at the edge of Daniel's workshop. Eventually, they'd form a gate for the Markham family.

"You shouldn't be doing Zach's work for him," Daniel drawled. "If he wants to slack, let him face the consequences."

There were lots of things that Evan could've said to that. Like, *"You do know that Zach's mother is sick, right?"* Or, *"Since I've known him 5 days and you've known him since childhood, you should be more eager to help than me."* Or maybe, *"Do you have any fucking conscience whatsoever?"*

Instead Evan said, "I'm done now, anyway."

Avoiding conflict was his mode of operation. They'd taught him that at basic training, once they'd figured out his hair-trigger temper. *Always avoid conflict.*

It worked, partly. Daniel nodded, and didn't say another word about Zach or the gate. But he did hover as Evan put away his equipment and checked the forge's temperature. And when Evan headed for the exit, Daniel was right on his heels.

"You walking?" Daniel asked, his long strides matching Evan's easily.

"Yep," Evan replied.

"It's been a long week. Let me drive you home."

"That's okay," Evan smiled. "I like to walk." It *was* true; he needed physical activity like he needed air. Plus, he had to be gentle with Daniel. It wouldn't do to alienate the boss's kid, even if that kid happened to be a grown man.

"Oh, come on." Daniel grinned back, a wide, white-toothed smile. Evan hadn't seen much of Ravenswood yet, but he'd seen enough to know that the small town's inhabitants adored Daniel Burne. And if he hadn't, the easy expectation in Daniel's green eyes would've made it clear. This man had never been told 'no', and never thought he would be.

Those were the men you had to watch.

"Alright," Evan relented as they broke out into the cool, evening air. It was just after five, so Ravenswood's streets were busy. Which meant that there was an old woman heading into the town centre on foot, and two Volvos making their way there via road.

"Great!" Daniel clapped Evan on the back, a firm slap that spoke of a camaraderie they had not forged. It was funny; in the army, that sort of immediate connection had come easy. But here, with this man, the familiarity set Evan's teeth on edge.

"I parked in town," Daniel said. "Just 'round the corner."

Evan nodded. Since 'town' referred to the centre of Ravenswood, and Ravenswood itself was about three miles long —surrounding farmland included— nothing was very far from anything else.

But Daniel managed to pack the next five minutes with a lifetime's worth of meaningless chatter anyway.

"So, where are you living? Those new flats?"

The flats had been built in 2015, but here in Ravenswood, that counted as new.

"Yep," Evan confirmed. "Elm Block." The town's habit of naming everything in sight was something he quite enjoyed.

Daniel, apparently, did not agree. His already-pale face

blanched slightly, his brow furrowed. "Serious?" he asked. "Elm?"

Something in his voice had changed. It was tight, strained, slightly scratchy.

Evan slowed down, his eyes focusing on Daniel with curiosity rather than veiled disdain. "Yeah. Why?"

"That's bad luck, mate," Daniel said. He nodded his head over and over again, disturbingly emphatic. "*Very* bad luck. I suppose you had no-one in town to guide you. There's some very shady characters living in Elm, you know."

Evan's brows flew up. "Shady characters?" he echoed. "In Ravenswood? I haven't been here long, but that doesn't sound right."

"Trust me," Daniel said darkly. "We all have our burdens to bear."

Evan bit back a snort. Apparently, he could add *Drama King* to the list of Daniel Burne's irritating qualities.

"Be careful," Daniel continued. "I'm just saying." Then he jerked his head towards a huge, blue BMW a few metres away, parked across two spaces. "That's mine."

Evan blinked at the monstrous thing for a moment, trying to come up with a compliment. He failed. To fill the silence, he returned to the ominous topic of his little block of flats.

"I only have one neighbour. Haven't met them yet, but I think it's someone elderly. They don't seem to leave the house."

"Hm," Daniel grunted. "Well—"

His sage wisdom was thankfully interrupted. As they neared the BMW, a small figure came rushing around a nearby corner and knocked right into them both.

Ruth entered the town car park with a lot on her mind. Major highlights included:

1. Her stomach cramps, which had gone from mild irritation to knuckle-biting pain in the space of twenty minutes.

2. The indignity of waddling about town with loo roll stuffed down her knickers.

3. The absolutely extortionate price she'd just paid for a packet of substandard tampons that didn't even have bloody applicators.

4. Mrs. Needham, newsagent proprietor and town gossip, who would tell everyone that Ruth had come in to buy tampons as if they were Year Eight children instead of grown adults.

5. How much the average person might know about the theory of relativity. Because, the less people knew about it, the more she could get away with fudging the details for the latest issue of her web comic.

Was it really surprising, with all that to ponder, that she ran headlong into a pair of enormous men?

Ruth landed on the tarmac with an unladylike grunt. At least it was more elegant than the word currently burning through her mind: *Motherfucker!*

This was to be imagined, you understand, as an outraged yowl of pain.

For an instant of blissful, foolish shock, Ruth blinked down at the ground. Then she looked up slightly, just a touch—enough to see two pairs of sturdy, boot-clad feet before her. The sight of those feet, along with her embarrassment, took Ruth from mildly irritated to unreasonably angry.

But *really*. Those boots were entirely too solid and quite abominably stable. The men hadn't even wobbled. They might at least pretend to be slightly unbalanced, since she was literally on the floor. Such firm uprightness in a situation like this struck her as rude.

"I'm so sorry," one of the men said. She didn't know which, because she refused to look up at their faces. She had quite enough to process right now without bringing faces and expressions and human lifeforms into it.

But one of the men, presumably the one who had spoken, ruined things completely by bending down to her level. He could do that, you see, because *he* hadn't fallen. The prick.

He crouched before her, bringing his faded jeans into view, and then his tight, black T-shirt—what a ridiculous outfit in February—and then... well, some rather interesting musculature.

That musculature broke through Ruth's haze of unreasonable annoyance, prodding her sharply. It said, *Look at that chest! Look at those biceps! You'd better check out his face, just to see if it's equally impressive. Quality control, and all that.*

Reigning in the urge to throw a temper tantrum—she was feeling fragile, what with the tissue in her knickers—Ruth looked up.

"Holy shit," she said.

The most beautiful man on Earth frowned at her. "Are you alright? Did you hit your head?"

Ruth didn't bother answering. Talking to this guy could not possibly be as worthwhile as simply looking at him. In fact, talking to him might ruin the effect. Or ruin her concentration, at least. So he continued to ask unanswered questions, and she continued to watch his lips move.

They looked soft. The thick, dirty-blonde beard covering his jaw looked soft too, matching the too-long hair falling over his brow. His bone structure, unlike his hair, didn't look soft at all. Nor did his furrowed brows or his piercing eyes, blue as a summer sky. Of course, skies were never blue in England—but she'd seen the sky in Sierra Leone, had spent hours staring up at it from her grandmother's garden. That was the best slice of sky on Earth, so she felt authorised to make the comparison.

The stranger's voice was raw and satisfying, threaded with something that might've been concern, and it soothed Ruth's embarrassment-induced irritation beautifully.

But then came a voice that brought it back ten-fold.

"Don't bother," said Daniel Burne. "She's slow."

Ruth's head snapped up, her gaze settling on the person she hated most in the world.

His smile was as cruel and as gorgeous as ever. For a moment, Ruth's heart lurched. But then she looked back at the stranger, who was still crouched beside her—who was *frowning* —and she felt slightly consoled.

The stranger was far more handsome than Daniel. How he must hate that.

Biting down on the inside of her cheek, Ruth stood. She ignored the fact that the tissue in her knickers felt slightly dislodged. She ignored the fact that there must be grit and dirt on her pyjama bottoms, and even ignored the fact that she was in her pyjamas at all, with only a jacket to hide them.

Ruth folded her arms across her chest and took a deep steadying breath, staring Daniel down. She said, "If I'm *slow*, what kind of man does that make you?"

His lip curled. "Opportunistic, perhaps."

Direct hit, of course. She'd expected nothing less.

Her jaw set, Ruth turned on her heel. Daniel wasn't worth talking to, anyway. He was beneath her notice. He was a gnat. But gnats were infuriating too, when you couldn't squash them.

"Wait!" the stranger called.

Ruth ignored him. She walked faster. She could see her car now, just a few metres away, gleaming like an oasis in the desert.

Then she heard the heavy footsteps of a man running behind her. "Miss!" he called. "You dropped your..."

Ruth stopped. Her hands balled into fists. She spat out, "For fuck's sake," and her breath twisted before her like smoke in the evening air.

The man was right behind her now. "I'm sorry," he said. He seemed to say that a lot.

She turned to face him. He really *did* look apologetic. Maybe because she'd fallen, maybe because Daniel was a prick, or maybe because he was holding out the box of tampons she'd dropped.

At the newsagent, Mrs. Needham had asked if she wanted a bag for five pence, and Ruth had thought, *Goodness me, five pence on a bag when I have two good hands?* And said, "No, thank you."

Now she was rather wishing she had parted with the five pence.

"Are you sure you're okay?" the man asked. "I'm sorry about... Daniel's behaviour." He said Daniel's name with the sort of tone she'd use to say *kitten killer*. Maybe that's what this gorgeous stranger thought: that Ruth was a kitten.

She snatched the tampons from him, turned her back, and walked away. He'd learn the truth soon enough.

The only question was—which truth?

Ruth started her engine and pulled out of the car park with almost reckless speed. Still, she wasn't fast enough to miss an intriguing tableau.

The stranger striding away from Daniel. Daniel shouting after him.

Ruth lowered her car window, just a touch, to catch the words.

Daniel called, "You're really pissed? Over a girl like her?"

A girl like her. It was a familiar phrase, especially from Daniel's lips.

But there was nothing familiar about the stranger. He tossed a glare over his shoulder and called back, "Don't worry about the lift. I'll walk."

———

A Girl Like Her is available now wherever books are sold.

Acknowledgments

This book has taken a long and higgledy-piggledy road to its current form. Since its birth in the Rogue Nights Anthology way back in 2018, James and Nina's story has undergone multiple transformations. Thank you to the countless readers who have supported them through it all.

Thank you to Kia Thomas for her fantastic editing. Major thanks to the whole team at Qamber Designs for a wonderful cover, and for putting up with my chaotic approach to design.

Finally, thank you to Louise Bay, Sabrina Bowen, Lauren Blakely, and all the other badass authors who helped get this baby back out into the world. You know who you are!

About the Author

Talia Hibbert is an award-winning and *New York Times* bestselling author who lives in a bedroom full of books. Supposedly, there is a world beyond that room, but she has yet to drum up enough interest to investigate.

Talia writes sexy, diverse romance because marginalised people deserve joyous representation, and also because she very much enjoys it. Follow her social media to connect, or email her directly at hello@taliahibbert.com.